THE DEMON UNDERTAKER

AN MM PARANORMAL ROMANCE

POSSESSIVE LOVE

ALEX J. ADAMS

To Jess

Best wishes

Alex J. Adams xx

First Edition

Editing: Karen Meeus

Cover Art: Charli Childs

Formatting: Delaney Rain Author Services

TRIGGER WARNING

Please note this book does deal with the grief associated with the death of a loved one and a terminal illness.

CHAPTER
ONE
MAL

H ey, Mal. Whatcha doing?"
My brother, Zeke, was nothing if not annoying.
"I'm busy. What do you want?" I glanced away from my computer screen to see him slouching in one of the comfortable chairs usually reserved for grieving friends and relatives, his leg thrown over one of the arms. He wore his usual dark jeans and polo shirt, not exactly a business suit, but he wasn't the one who dealt with the general public.

"Ooh, someone got out of bed on the wrong side this morning," he teased.

"Spit it out, Zeke. I've got work to do. So have you, actually." I hated it when he disturbed me for no apparent reason.

"You need to lighten up," he said. "There's more to life than death, you know."

"Not for us, there isn't. It's our business, remember?" I reminded him.

Dad had already been onto me this morning. We were down on our quota of souls for the week. Who knew that reaping souls was such a corporate business these days?

For fuck's sake. I couldn't make them die. We'd already tried to increase our odds by moving to the arse end of

England, a place notorious for an ageing population. Short of going out and committing murder, I wasn't sure what else I could do.

"Jeez, you take everything so seriously. Chill the fuck out, Mal." He straightened up in the chair, realising I was in no mood to be fucked around this morning.

I sighed. "What was it you wanted?"

My patience was dwindling fast.

"Yanni and me, we're going out later. Wondered if you wanted to join us. He says he has a proposition that could benefit us."

Yanni was a second cousin, twice removed or something like that, and was shady as shit.

Zeke and me? We weren't exactly squeaky clean, but we tried not to bring attention to ourselves or the business. The last thing we needed was the fucking police hanging around investigating an unnatural amount of deaths.

Believe me, it wouldn't be the first time that had happened. We'd learnt to be invisible. Well, as inconspicuous as two demons could be, roaming around the south of England.

Slow and steady was our motto.

Actually, it wasn't.

Bury the bodies—reap the souls.

That was our motto. Our unofficial motto. Can you imagine having that above the door or on our website?

We'd be shut down for sure, but it was, in fact, what we did.

Perfect Shores Funeral Parlour was a front for our other business, the collection of souls.

We were the kind of demons that didn't think twice about sending ungrateful, sorry souls down to Hell where all the damned humans belonged.

I loathed and detested every one of them. No exceptions.

Zeke, on the other hand, loved them all. A little too much if the noises from his bedroom were anything to go by. A steady parade of men and women almost every night, no matter how much I asked him to take his 'business' elsewhere.

I had no time for that, more than content to be on my own for all eternity. I was a loner. I needed no one.

"He's bad news, Zeke," I told him.

"We're demons. We're all bad news," he countered.

Well, yes, he had me there, and maybe what Yanni was offering was something we could use, although I very much doubted it.

"Come on, Malcolm. You know you want to." Zeke laughed, knowing I hated when he used my full name.

"Don't fucking call me that." He got the cool name. Ezekiel.

I got fucking Malcolm. Hardly a name for a kick-ass demon! I didn't know what my mother had been thinking, giving me that name. She'd argued that in French, Mal meant evil. It was a fitting name, she said. That might well be true, but Malcolm wasn't.

I sat for a moment and thought about what Yanni could offer us. It couldn't hurt to listen.

"I'll give him an hour, no more, and if I don't like his plan, we don't do it. Get it?" I knew what Zeke was like. He was easily talked into shit, especially by Yanni. I'd bailed his arse out on more than one occasion over the centuries, and every time, he was with that waste of space, Yanni.

Why was I even giving him the time of day, one might ask. I was contemplating that myself, but business was slow. It was summer, and they weren't dying as quickly as in the winter when the cold weather and influenza hit.

I needed something; I just didn't like going to Yanni for the solution to my problem. I didn't want to be indebted to him in any way, shape or form.

"So, you'll come then?" Zeke seemed far too excited, and I wondered if he knew what Yanni wanted to discuss. Now I was really worried!

"I'll be there. The Old Swan, yes? Meet me there at seven, no later, else I'll be gone," I told him.

He stood from his chair and saluted. "Yes, sir! No later than seven. Get the beers in if you're there before we are."

"Get out, Zeke. Go do something useful, like find some souls to reap."

"On it."

He left the room, slamming the door behind him.

What did I ever do to deserve a brother like him? He was a reckless dick at times, but he did pull his weight when it mattered. I didn't always ask where the bodies came from; sometimes it was easier living in the dark.

As much as I liked it here, I was getting a little bored. There wasn't much to do for a centuries-old demon that had not already been done. Whereas Zeke was happy to play on his mobile phone and his Xbox, that didn't interest me at all.

I read. Some of my oldest friends were authors: Agatha Christie, Charles Dickens and my personal favourite, Sir Arthur Conan Doyle. We had some fun chatting about Sherlock. Some of his finest ideas came from me, although he'd never told anyone that.

I wanted a challenge, something to sink my teeth into. Not literally, although I'd been known to do that a time or two.

Maybe it was time to move on. If this thing, whatever it was, didn't pan out with Yanni, I'd speak to Dad about finding me something else. I was losing my edge being here.

Let's face it, I was bored as fuck.

THREE MINUTES past seven and they still hadn't arrived. Zeke knew what a stickler I was for time. He also knew it would wind me the fuck up, him being late. I swear Dad sent him here to fuck with me.

The patience of a saint, that's what I had, which was pretty ironic really. I'd never been a saint, and I doubted I ever would be. Not unless they changed the criteria pretty quickly.

I downed my drink, intent on leaving, when the door swung open and in walked Zeke and Yanni, laughing at something or other as usual.

"Yo, Malcolm!" Yanni shouted when he spotted me. "How's it hanging?"

I rolled my eyes, trying desperately to hide.

He threw himself into the chair next to me and picked up a drink from the table, chugging it down before belching loudly.

"Fuck, that's better. Been dying for a pint all day."

"So, what's this proposition you have? Zeke said it could benefit us."

"Are we having another beer? I could really do with one." Yanni stood, swaying slightly.

"Sit. Tell me. Then you can go to the bar." Being here in a room full of humans was not my ideal way to spend an evening.

"Jeez, someone needs to chill," Yanni said.

"That's what I told him," Zeke said, and I glared in his direction, silencing him.

"Look, just keep your voice down. We don't need the population of this godforsaken town knowing all of our business."

"Yeah, well. I've got a couple of things going on you might be interested in. I've heard a few things on the grapevine about how collection numbers are dropping. It's a worldwide thing."

"I know, but what can _you_ do about it?"

"I have this contact. Says he knows where he can get souls with no questions asked."

Most demons would probably jump at the chance to not have to do any work to reap souls, for them to just fall in their lap with no work whatsoever. Most demons had no conscience and couldn't care less where souls came from.

I was slightly different. I wasn't a fan of humans, never had been, but it didn't mean I wanted them killed just to get the numbers up. I played by the rules. The problem was, if we killed and reaped for the hell of it, soon enough, there'd be nothing left. There had to be a balance.

I knew whatever Yanni had to offer wasn't good, and right now, bringing attention to us was *no*t the way to go.

"I'm not interested, Yanni. Sounds like more trouble than it's worth. What else do you have?"

"Eh, your loss. There's others interested anyway. I thought I'd give you the heads-up. You're my best demon, Mal. You know this."

"You said a couple of things." I was eager to move this along. The less time I spent with this guy, the better.

"Oh, yeah. I have a new contact for paperwork. You know, for disappearances."

"What happened to the last guy?" Zeke asked what I was already thinking.

"Best you don't know. He pissed off the wrong person, and now he's, erm, no longer around."

That was a shame. He'd been quick, efficient and never caused us any bother. Breaking in another human would be a tedious job. Maybe I should leave it to Zeke.

"Well, if there's nothing else?" I stood, ready to leave. That was me done for the day. I was ready to go home, pour myself a glass of whisky and listen to some music.

A prickle of something uncomfortable skittered down my back, and I spun around, scanning the room. It usually signified another demon in the vicinity, and not always a nice one. Zeke must have felt it too, as he did he same.

"You feel that?" he asked me quietly.

"Yeah, I do." I looked again but saw nothing out of the

ordinary. Everyone appeared to be as they should, but that meant nothing.

If anyone looked at us, they'd see three tall, well-built men having a quiet drink. Yet, any demon worth his salt would know what we were.

"I'm going home, but watch yourself, Zeke. I don't trust whatever that was."

"Nah, me neither. You take care going home too."

I snorted. I was six feet three and built like a brick shithouse. No human could take me, and very few demons could. Despite my name, I was one of the most powerful demons around. I just didn't advertise the fact.

"See you later, and be quiet tonight. I would like to get some sleep."

Zeke laughed, breaking the tension. "I can't promise that. I'm a lover, not a fighter."

I shook my head and nodded to Yanni and left the pub. I wish I could say the sensation of being watched left me, but I could still feel it as I walked to my car. They, too, must have been a demon of some note to elicit such a response in me. Normal, lower-grade demons didn't usually register.

I was tempted to call out to them but thought it would be better in the end if I didn't advertise the fact I knew they were there.

Scuffling behind me made me cautious, and I picked up the pace. My keys rattled as I took them out of my pocket in readiness. Defending myself wasn't an issue; I just didn't want to have to do it in the middle of a street in summer.

Finally reaching my car, I got in and locked the doors, checking my surroundings. The sensation disappeared, and I breathed a sigh of relief.

I pulled out my phone and called Zeke.

"The minute you left, so did 'it', whatever it was. There's nothing now."

"Same here. It definitely followed me to the car, but it's gone now. We need to be vigilant."

I hung up and started the car. Time to go home.

Something was coming. I just didn't know what or when.

If it wanted to wait, then that's what we'd do.

CHAPTER
TWO
JASON

T t's time to move on, Jase. It's been eighteen months now."
My friend, Kristine, sat on the other side of the table from me in the local coffee shop. We came here almost every day, and I listened to her say the exact same thing almost every day.

I gave her the same answer. "I'm not ready. I can't move on yet."

"One of these days, you'll tell me, yes, you can move on," she said, casually swirling the coffee in her mug.

"Today is not that day, though, is it?" I snapped, not remotely in the mood for her compassion today.

"You know I'm always here for you, but you need to start trying to get your life back on track. It's been too long."

"So you keep saying, but how can you tell me how long I need to grieve for? Kieran was my world. You know this." My eyes stung as they usually did when I thought of him.

We should have grown old together, had a family and lived a happy life. Instead, we'd had five beautiful years until an aggressive cancer had taken him sooner than we thought was possible. We'd barely had time to arrange the funeral before he was gone, leaving me alone and mourning the loss of the other half of my heart.

He was irreplaceable. I'd never find another like him, but according to Kristine, I should at least be out there looking.

That was never going to happen. I was content to die a widower. No one could replace him, ever.

She reached out and covered my hand with hers.

"I just worry about you, Jase. You barely eat, you never go out other than to work, and when was the last time you had a shave and a haircut?"

I might have let myself go a little since he'd died, I'd admit. It had been months before I had even been able to leave the house. I'd lie around playing his favourite music, rarely sleeping or eating. I became a shadow of my former self. If it hadn't been for an intervention by Kristine and my family, I was sure I'd still be there.

I pushed them away for so long, until eventually, I knew I needed help.

Getting back to work was the first step. We'd run a little antiques shop in Edgmund-on-Sea, a small seaside town in the south of England. It wasn't as popular as some of the surrounding towns, but we did okay. Admittedly, the average age of the population was about eighty, or at least it seemed to be, but trade was good and both Kieran and I had loved it.

Now, I ran it with Kristine, bless her. She'd given up her job to help me out, picking up the slack when I couldn't. When the debilitating grief would overwhelm me, sometimes lasting days, sometimes weeks.

"I'm sorry, it's just one of those days today." A day where I'd barely made it out of bed.

"I know, and I'm sorry, babe, but let's do what we can, eh?" She checked her watch and quickly gulped her coffee down. "Drink up. It's almost time to open the shop."

I didn't see the point in rushing. We rarely got any customers before midday. The town didn't seem to wake up until then, but she insisted we be there before ten to open up.

"I'll take mine to go. I'm nowhere near done." I signalled to the young barista, Harry, and he grabbed a to-go cup in readiness.

I glanced in the mirror behind the counter, wondering who the hell that scruffy homeless person was behind me. With a heavy heart, I realised that was me. Maybe Kristine was right. I needed to get a haircut and a shave.

As we left the shop, I handed her the keys.

"You're right about one thing. I do need a haircut and a shave. I'm going to nip into the barber's a few streets along, get myself tidied up a little."

She pinched both my cheeks, making kissy noises. "You know it's the right thing to do, Jason, and you'll feel much better. Take your time. I'll watch the shop."

I shook my head at her. It was just a haircut, but I could see how she'd be pleased with that. I really had let myself go.

A few minutes later, I was pushing open the door of the barber's shop. The man that owned it had had it for forever, from what I'd been told.

"Take a seat, son. I'll be with you shortly." I chuckled to myself. Son... I was thirty-five, hardly a boy.

I took a seat on the worn leather bench in the window and picked up a magazine from the small table. It looked as old as the shop. I flicked through it lazily, not really paying attention, more interested in my surroundings.

There were two chairs, one occupied by a large man with a full head of thick, blond curly hair and a beard, sipping a mug of something hot. He turned and smiled at me, blue eyes twinkling. Maybe in a different time and place, it might have affected me.

"I'll wait, Arthur. You take care of this gentleman. I'll just finish my tea."

Arthur gestured to the chair, and I made myself comfortable while he wrapped a cape around my shoulders.

I really was a mess, I thought to myself as I looked at my reflection in the mirror, and judging by the look on Arthur's face, he thought so too.

"Mmm, it's been a while since the last haircut," he said, combing it through.

I nodded. "Yeah, I was, erm, not feeling myself and kind of neglected it a little."

Understatement of the year, but if it kept Kristine off my back, I'd do it. While I wasn't 'moving on', as she put it, some effort needed to be made.

"Well, we'll have you looking handsome in no time."

He started to cut, and I watched with interest, seeing the old me slowly re-emerge.

"What's the plan for today?" Arthur's words startled me out of my thoughts.

"Erm, just work? I own the antiques store on the front, All That Glitters."

"Ah, yes. I think I've been there a time or two. Lovely young lady works there, but what happened to the other man that worked there? It's been a while since I've seen him."

"My husband died." It didn't get any easier saying those words.

He stopped cutting and caught my eye in the mirror. "I'm so very sorry to hear that. Please accept my condolences."

"Thank you, but it's been almost eighteen months."

"Doesn't matter how long it's been. My Clara has been gone for ten years, and I still miss her."

He resumed and snipped here and there, making me look more human.

"Hot towel shave, sir?"

"Call me Jason, and yes, that would be great."

Arthur stepped into the back of the store, leaving me alone

with the blond-haired man.

"Still hurts, doesn't it?" he said matter-of-factly.

I eyed him in the mirror as he hugged his mug, and I nodded.

"I can help," he whispered.

"I don't need a therapist." I'd visited one shortly after Kieran's death but to no avail. I'd felt no comfort from their words, but in actuality, I probably didn't want to be helped, still raw from his passing.

"Who said anything about therapy? Tell Arthur I'll be back later. I've some errands I need to run."

He stood and placed his mug on the shelf by the mirror, then dug around in his pocket. He pulled out a card and handed it to me.

"Call me." I took it, reading the name that seemed to quiver and pulse.

ZEKE

I turned it over in my hand. Just a number on the back. There was no address, nothing. How strange. I tucked it into my pocket just as Arthur returned with the towels, and for the next twenty minutes, I was pampered like never before.

Although the man staring back at me from the mirror was infinitely more human, I was still shocked by my appearance. With no beard to hide my face, I realised how much weight I'd lost. I looked gaunt and pale, with dark circles beneath my eyes.

I still wasn't ready to move on, but baby steps, and this was the first one.

"Oh, look at you all handsome!" Kristine said as she rushed over to hug me. "You look great."

"I look skinny as fuck, and I can't breathe!"

"Sorry, sorry," she muttered as she let me go. She took my hands and held me at arm's length. "Give me a twirl."

"No twirling. It's just a haircut."

"And a shave." She swiped at a tear. "You look good, Jason. You'll get there."

Whatever. It was just a haircut. I walked over to some boxes piled over by the door.

"New delivery? I didn't think we had anything else coming in for a while?"

"Oh, yeah. I ordered a few things last week. I didn't think you'd mind."

I didn't particularly care if I was honest. The past few months, I'd been considering closing the shop down completely. Everything here reminded me of him, right down to the coffee mug that still sat in the cupboard in the kitchen.

"It's fine." I opened the nearest box and took out the first item on the top. I unwrapped it and revealed a beautiful glass vase. A rainbow reflected on the wall behind me as I held it up to the light. Once upon a time, I would have oohed and aahed with Kieran over its craftsmanship, but now it was just another trinket to add to those on the tables.

We didn't have traditional shelves. Most of the items were placed on tables scattered around the shop. It made for better browsing, Kieran had always said. Only our most precious pieces were kept in glass cabinets, away from the sticky fingers of children and thieves.

"Also, Mrs Peters passed away." I could tell Kristine was reluctant to tell me. She always was when the subject of death arose. "You remember her son, Brendan? He said he'll be by at some point to talk about her possessions. There might be some things of interest we could buy from him."

I didn't like Brendan. Even when Kieran was alive, he'd flirt with me, and while Kieran thought it was funny, I thought it was just damn rude.

"I'll make sure I'm out. You can deal with him." I stalked into the back room and over to my desk. "I have some paperwork to catch up on."

I knew I was being an arsehole, and Kristine had been more than patient and understanding, but sometimes I wanted to wallow in my own misery. Today was one of those days.

She didn't answer, used to my pissy moods by now, as was her wife, Sam. I'd been selfish at a time when they needed me. They were expecting their first child very soon.

The computer took an age to turn on, and I remembered the card I'd stashed in my pocket earlier.

I pulled it out, again curious as to how the shimmering bronze letters seemed to throb.

It was becoming apparent I did need some sort of help. Perhaps this was the guy to help me.

Toying with it, I turned it over and over in my hand while the computer booted up. I could google the number. Maybe that would give me some information.

"Finally," I muttered as the screen loaded, and I quickly opened the search engine, typing in his name and number.

Nothing. Not that it was strange, but I'd hoped something would turn up.

I threw it to the side and opened up my emails. I tried to concentrate, replying to ones from auction houses and prospective customers wanting to know how much they could get for their 'antiques'.

While some were genuine, I was quite sure most were worthless items bought at car boot sales. Either way, my attention was constantly drawn to the unobtrusive card on the desk.

"Zeke, Zeke, Zeke." I repeated the name several times and hoped for some insight, getting nothing.

Coffee. That's what I needed.

Kristine was standing by the window on her mobile, speaking quietly.

"I know, Sam. I just don't know how much longer I can keep doing this. It's killing me, seeing him like this. It's been eighteen months."

It didn't take a genius to realise who she was talking about. I left her to it and went to the kitchen to make a pot of coffee. Kieran drank coffee like it was going out of fashion. I'd be content with a couple in the morning, preferring something less caffeinated in the afternoon.

It always affected my sleep but had no such effect on him. He'd sleep like the dead.

Well, fuck. He did now.

Coffee finally brewed, I returned to my office.

Zeke. He said he could help. Why was I so fixated on the stupid card?

I picked it up again, unable to explain the effect it was having on me.

I took my phone from my pocket. A photo of Kieran and his exquisite smile captivated me, as it always did on my phone, and I paused to gaze at it, touching the screen ever so lightly.

Did I want to get over him? I didn't think I did, but I was being selfish. He was dead, I was living, as was everyone else around me. They'd come to terms with his passing, and while I didn't think I ever would, Kristine was right. I should at least try to get on with my life without him in it.

I dialled the number before I could hang up and chicken out. It was answered on the third ring.

"Jason. I've been expecting your call."

How the fuck did he know it was me?

I paused for a moment, tempted to end the call. I finally plucked up the courage and spoke.

"You said you could help me. I want to know how."

"It's not for everyone, Jason, but I get the feeling you might be interested in what I have to say."

"Go on. I'm listening."

I sat at my desk and waited, definitely not expecting the next words out of his mouth.

"I can bring him back to you."

T he buzzer on the door sounded, which was strange. The bereaved usually made an appointment, and it was rare to get walk-ins, especially where we were situated in the town. While we wanted the business, we weren't exactly on a well-travelled thoroughfare.

Most of our business came from nursing homes and the local hospital. We had contacts, and our prices were on the cheap side, but that was because we were more interested in the souls than making money. That was no object to us.

We'd been around for centuries and had already amassed a fortune we could never hope to spend.

It was always, always about the souls.

I'd already had one appointment this morning and had reached my tolerance for humans for the day. I could only stand so many. Their moaning and whining grated on every last nerve I possessed, but I'd put on my best consoling face and deal with whoever was here.

Death was death. Death was inevitable. I didn't see what all the fuss was about.

I'd complained to Dad and told him Zeke was far more suitable for the role of frontman. For some strange reason known only to him, he insisted it needed to be me. Something about me having kind, compassionate eyes.

Utter fucking bullshit. I'm surprised most humans didn't see through me into the darkness I carried inside of me.

I hated humans, every single one of them.

"Be nice," Dad had said. "They're our business."

I'd yet to meet one I liked.

Where the fuck was Zeke? He could deal with this one, but as usual, he was nowhere to be found.

I stood and fastened the button on my jacket. I smoothed down my hair, took a deep breath and stepped into the reception area.

"Can I help you?"

The face that greeted me was one of sorrow. Nothing I hadn't seen before, but for some reason, this one resonated with me.

His eyes were red and swollen. His clothes hung from a too thin frame.

Poor guy, he must have lost someone very close to him and possibly recently.

I held out my hand and introduced myself.

"Hi. I'm Mal. The undertaker."

He took my proffered hand and shook it firmly. The frisson that passed between us took both of us by surprise.

"I'm Jason," he said, dropping his hand from mine. "Sorry, that's always happening."

Not to me it didn't, but I refused to read anything into it.

"Is there something I can help you with, Jason? Do you have someone you need to bury or cremate?"

I know, I know. My bedside manner needed work.

"I was looking for Zeke?" he said, glancing around the room.

Of course he was. Was he one of his conquests or someone for the other business we ran?

"He's not here right now. Anything I can help you with?"

He looked around again, refusing to meet my gaze. They always felt guilty about wanting to bring their loved ones back to life.

Zeke's conquests were normally more confident than this one.

"He, erm, gave me his card?" Finally, he looked at me, and I didn't miss the bone-deep grief on his face.

Definitely one of his other clients. According to Zeke, where his sex life was concerned, his dick was his calling card.

"You could leave your details, and I can ask him to call you."

"I don't know." He was losing his nerve, ready to bolt. I couldn't let him do that.

"Please," I said, taking his elbow. Both of us jumped as that same shock of electricity passed through us. "Come into my office. I'll take some details and pass them on to Zeke."

Reluctantly, he allowed me to guide him to the office and into one of the easy chairs Zeke had been lounging in only the day before.

"Can I get you a drink?" I was never this nice to humans, but for some reason, I felt compelled to put him at ease.

"I'm fine, thank you. I can come back, or you can just get Zeke to call me. I don't want to disturb you. You're probably really busy."

"It's no problem, really. Why don't you tell me a little about yourself, why you want Zeke's services."

I'd usually leave all this to Zeke. His business was just that, his business.

"How do you know Zeke?" He seemed a little more relaxed now. I was confident he'd stay.

"He's my brother. We run this place together."

"So you know what he offered me."

I nodded. I knew about his sideline.

"Eighteen months ago, I lost my husband to cancer. One minute he was fine, the next he was gone. It was all so sudden."

There was that sad look again, but I waited for him to gather his composure and continue his story.

"You don't need to hear all this, surely."

"Please, go on. This is all vital information." It wasn't, but what would make a seemingly sane man pay the money I knew Zeke asked for this service to bring back a loved one? How desperate did you need to be?

He fidgeted in his chair. This couldn't be easy for him, but why did I care? What the hell did it matter to me?

"We had five years together. We filled the last one with doctor and hospital appointments, pointless chemotherapy sessions that did fuck all. Sorry for swearing. Not something I usually do."

"I get it. Cancer can be brutal and take our loved ones when we least expect it."

He shrugged. "What can you do? This was aggressive. We hardly had any time to prepare, barely enough time to say goodbye."

At this point in a story, I'd usually be losing interest and have to feign concern in the remainder, but the man sitting in front of me held my attention.

"My friend, Kristine, keeps telling me it's time to move on. I just can't. I can't let him go. I won't let him go."

He looked me in the eye as he uttered those final words, and it hit me right in the gut.

"Sometimes it's for the best," I suggested, but he shook his head.

"No, not this time. He shouldn't have died. He wasn't even thirty. Old people die."

I knew that wasn't the case, and I also knew that even though we could bring people back from the dead, it wasn't indefinitely. Resurrection only lasted for a year, a little longer if they were lucky and had the money.

If we brought his husband back, he'd be in the exact same

state when he died again. And for some strange reason I could not fathom, I didn't want that for him.

"Maybe your friend is right," I told him.

He stood and headed for the door. "Just tell your brother I was here. I still want to talk to him."

"Look, Jason. I didn't mean…"

He threw a card on my desk. "My number. Give it to him."

Before I could say anything else, he walked out of the office, the front door buzzing again as it opened and closed.

"Fucking hell," I cursed, kicking my feet up on the desk.

That couldn't have gone worse if I'd have wanted it to. Why the hell was I bothered by this? If Zeke wasn't around, I'd usually take a few details, take their money, and then pass it over to him to deal with the rest of it.

I was the admin guy. He did the dirty work of resurrecting them. No way I was sullying my expensive suits, digging up bodies or getting dusty with ashes.

Sometimes, I was happy to be the frontman.

I picked up my phone and called Zeke.

"Where the fuck are you?" I asked when he answered the phone.

"I'm working." A woman's laughter tinkled in the background, and I could only guess what kind of work he was doing.

"Get your arse back here. A job's come in."

I didn't need to tell him anything else. He'd know what I meant. I ended the call and picked up the card from my desk.

Jason Barr,
Owner
All That Glitters Antique Store.

I wasn't sure I knew that one, but then I didn't know everyone in town.

I needed to get out of these clothes and stretch my legs, literally. My skin was getting as uncomfortable as my suit right now.

I locked the front door, then went downstairs into the basement, stripping off my suit as I went until I was down to my boxers.

I locked the door behind me and threw my clothes on the chair in the corner.

I rolled my shoulders and tilted my neck from side to side, releasing the kinks. I took a deep breath and stretched my hands out in front of me. My fingers lengthened, long pointed nails growing out of each one.

This was just the beginning of my transformation from human to demon. It didn't hurt. In fact, it was always a relief to be in my natural form. I didn't have a tail, and I definitely didn't have hooves.

I grew another six inches in height and gained about another fifty pounds of muscle. I was a big fucker, definitely bigger than Zeke. Another bone of contention between me and my brother.

I braced myself and bent forward to lean on a small table set in the middle of the room as grey, leathery wings sprouted from between my shoulder blades, the tips sweeping the floor. Short, black, twisted horns sprouted from my head.

Fuck, that felt good. Better than good, actually.

I shook out my wings and realised it had been some time since I'd shifted. I knew for a fact Zeke shifted almost every night. He preferred having sex as a demon and usually wiped memories before kicking them out of his bed. He would just leave them with the memory of a fantastic night, but one he never repeated.

Sex wasn't on my agenda. It had been a good few years since I'd had any interest in it, much to Zeke's amusement. He thought there was something wrong with me. It was more to do with having been burned, literally, many years before.

I didn't want to put myself through that again, and casual

sex wasn't really my thing. All that was available were humans unless I returned to the other realm, and I'd not done that in decades. As much as I loathed humans, I detested demons even more.

But I was an aggressive lover. I enjoyed biting, fucking and a compliant partner, not necessarily in that order.

And now, the thought was in my head. An image of a willing, writhing body beneath me, taking all I had to offer, left me with a tightness in my boxers.

I removed them, kicking them to the side, my erection bouncing in front of me. How long had it been since I'd even touched myself? I did not know, but the compulsion to do it now overtook all of my thoughts.

Pearls of precum dripped steadily from the end, pooling on the floor in front of me. I gripped my dick and squeezed hard enough to hurt.

A growl built in my chest as a surge of lust flooded through my body, and I staggered to keep my balance. I couldn't do this at work. It felt so wrong and so right, but this was neither the time nor the place, as much as I wanted this.

I made up my mind when I heard the thump of feet above me. Zeke was back.

I furled my wings and absorbed them back into my body, the same with my horns. With a little more concentration, I returned to my human size, still tall at six feet three.

I dressed quickly and ran back up the stairs, where Zeke was waiting for me.

"Why were you down there? You never go into the basement," he said with a smirk.

"I had something to do down there." I wasn't going to tell him I was about to have a wank thinking about a human. Was I thinking about a human? Was Jason the reason for my shift?

There was no way such a brief encounter would elicit such a response in me. That was just ridiculous.

"What was so urgent you had to call me away from a new client?"

I snorted. Client my arse.

"A man came to visit while you were 'meeting' your new female client. Jason Barr? He said you offered to do a resurrection."

"I might have mentioned it in passing," Zeke said noncommittally.

I rolled my eyes at him. "You gave him your card, dickhead. Usually means you've had more than a passing conversation with him."

"I met him in Arthur's place. He got talking, and I offered him our service. I guess I forgot he was coming in today. Did you get everything from him?"

"He left before I could get what we needed."

"So he didn't pay or sign any contracts?"

"No, he didn't." And honestly, I didn't want him to do any of that. I didn't want Zeke to perform the resurrection. "I got his card, though."

By now, we were back in my office, and I handed him the card Jason had left.

"I'm not sure he's a suitable candidate, though." I got the feeling he'd do anything to bring him back.

"Since when did we decide who was a fit candidate? As long as they have the money. We've never been fussy before."

Trying to explain my reluctance to go ahead with this one was hard. I rarely gave a shit.

"Perhaps we should think about this before we go rushing in headlong."

"Are you really Malcolm? The brother I know wouldn't normally give a rat's ass who we bring back to life. I wonder why this one's different? Anyone would think you had a heart."

Zeke tucked the card into the pocket of his shirt and turned to leave.

"I'll call him and set something up."

"You do that."

It was just after two in the afternoon, and I was done for the day. My human quota was more than full today.

I locked up as I left and climbed into my Aston Martin. It had been an extravagant purchase, but I had no regrets.

Our home was half an hour outside of town, a large six-bedroom property set in a couple of acres of well-manicured gardens and grounds. We liked our privacy to do what we wanted.

The journey was uneventful, and the six-foot wrought-iron gates swung open as I approached. I drove up the long driveway with trees on either side that led to a gravelled area in front of the house.

I parked the Aston in my usual spot and sat in the car for a moment, mentally preparing myself for the onslaught I was about to encounter.

My feet crunched on the gravel, announcing my arrival. I opened the front door, hearing nails clicking on the vintage black-and-white tiled floor before they skidded to a halt in front of me.

With ears back and a huge smile, our hellhound, Smokefang —Smokey, for short—waited, ready to pounce at any moment.

"Calm, Smokey. Don't you dare," I warned, my hands held out in front of me.

Not listening to a word, he jumped up and placed his front paws on my shoulders, licking my face. Yep, he was a gigantic dog, but considering he should have been vicious, from deep in the depths of Hell, he was as soft as a brush.

"You'll be the death of me, Smokey," I said, ruffling his fur. Dad said we spoilt him. I disagreed.

But maybe we should hide him away next time Dad visited.

"Mrs Gold?" I called out as Smokey bounded away.

"In the kitchen, dearie," she shouted.

I walked in to see her feeding Smokey a fresh heart. Even seated, his head came to her chest.

"I'll be going out for dinner tonight, so no need to cook. Zeke will be out until later. Why don't you get off home and spend some time with Mr Gold?"

"You're a kind man, Malcolm." Okay, so only she could call me that and get away with it. "I'll just finish up, then I'll be off."

I grabbed her coat and bag from by the door and ushered her out. She removed her apron as she went.

"Home, now. It looks like rain, and you should get home before it starts."

I watched as she hurried to her car and drove away.

Finally, I had the place to myself. I wondered what I could do with that time?

CHAPTER
FOUR
JASON

W hat's wrong, Jason?" Kristine asked as I walked back into the shop.

I wasn't sure. I felt strange, confused even. I'd gone to speak to Zeke with the intention of having Kieran brought back to me, but instead, I'd encountered an immense man—in height, stature and character.

What were Mal and Zeke? Certainly not human if they were able to bring back the dead. I'd been so focused on the possibility of having Kieran back with me, I'd not stopped to even think about how that was going to happen.

Kristine couldn't know. She'd encouraged me to move on, so there was no way she would understand my reasons for what I planned to do.

"I'm fine. An odd day is all." Odd indeed.

"Well, I thought we could go out later. You, me and Sam. Just for dinner, nothing more. There's a new restaurant opened close to here."

My reluctance to go must have shown on my face. After today, I wanted to go home and relax with a glass or two of wine, not sit in a restaurant and make small talk.

Kristine and Sam had been there for me, and the way I'd

acted today, perhaps a night out, just the three of us, would be fine.

"Okay," I conceded, "but I don't want to be out all evening."

Kristine beamed. "Sam said I wouldn't be able to convince you."

"You didn't convince me. I need to eat, and I suppose you're my closest friends. Plus, I've been a shit person lately."

She stood and walked over to me, her arms outstretched. Stepping into them, I sank into her warmth.

"Jesus, Jason. You're skin and bone." She held me closer and forced the air from my lungs. "You lost your husband. You're entitled to have bad days, but you have to come back to us. Losing Kieran was bad enough. I won't lose you too."

As usual, she made perfect sense. I was still going to try harder to be a better person.

"Now," she said, pleased with herself, "go home, get showered and changed. Sam and I will pick you up around six. Go on, be off with you."

She ushered me out of the door I'd just stepped through, and I found myself back on the street. The door shut behind me, and the sign turned to closed. I guessed I was done for the day.

Traffic in town had me detouring past Perfect Shores just as Mal was climbing into an Aston Martin. Of course he'd have one of those. I snorted. Rich bastards and their cars. Death must pay well.

Home wasn't too far away, and I arrived ten minutes later. Dread loomed as I unlocked the front door and stepped into the empty house.

Plagued by thoughts of Kieran, I walked into the bedroom we'd shared. It had taken me six months to step back into the room. By that time, Kristine and Kieran's brother had cleared out all of his belongings. I didn't know where they were, but they'd assured me that when the time was right, I could go through them and choose what I wanted to keep.

That was not gonna happen. He was coming back, and he'd need his stuff.

After another six months, I'd managed to sit in the room without bursting into floods of tears, remembering every night we'd spent there as lovers.

I still couldn't sleep in the bed we'd shared. Kristine had offered to change it, but I refused. We'd moved my clothes into the spare room, and that was where I now slept, in a single bed. On my own because that was how I spent my life now.

Alone.

His shoes were no longer by the front door, his glasses no longer sat on the nightstand, and his scent no longer lingered on the sheets.

All traces of him had gone...forever.

Did I have the right to bring him back? Was I selfish to want to do that?

I missed him like I'd miss my next breath.

I'd lived in a void for so long I didn't know how to climb out, but the question I'd been asking myself lately was if I wanted to escape the void.

The temptation to shut myself away with my memories grew with each passing day. Was it a coincidence that I'd met Zeke? Was it a sign from Kieran of what I needed to do? Was he talking to me from beyond the grave?

It seemed farcical, far-fetched, but what if it were true? What if I was meant to do this?

On the other hand, how the hell would I explain his return? We'd watched him waste away within a few months. He'd gone from a fit and healthy twenty-nine-year-old to a man so weak he could hardly lift a finger.

I'd remained strong for him, but the moment he'd passed, I crumpled, unable to feed or look after myself for months. With him by my side again, I'd be complete.

I looked over at the clock and realised I only had half an hour until Kristine arrived. How long had I been sitting here?

Time flew when I thought of Kieran. I'd think it'd been minutes, but hours would have passed. Today was no exception.

Kristine was never late. I'd really need to get a move on to be ready in time. I showered quickly and stood in front of my wardrobe, looking for something to wear. Something that wouldn't emphasise the huge amount of weight I'd lost.

I spied a pair of grey trousers at the back of the closet I'd bought years ago. I'd convinced myself at the time that I could squeeze into them. With all the weight I'd lost since Kieran had died, they'd fit perfectly.

I at least had a couple of shirts that were suitable. When I'd returned to work, Kristine had insisted I needed to wear something better than a scruffy T-shirt.

The doorbell rang just as I slipped on my shoes.

"Coming," I shouted, and I opened the door to see her standing there, her hair and make-up perfect. She'd turned many men's heads, but she had eyes only for her partner, Sam.

I grabbed my keys and phone and closed the door behind me. We ran to the car just as the heavens opened. I hopped in the back of the car and allowed Kristine to get in the front.

"Hey, Sam. Thanks for driving."

"Jason," she said, "it's good to see you out and about. Been far too long."

It'd been a couple of months since I'd seen her last, and she was blooming.

"How many more months?"

"Three, but I'm sure you know that."

I did know that, and I was so pleased for my friends, expecting their first child. Losing Kieran had taken the shine off the world for me, and all I could see was the darkness of grief and despair.

I should make more of an effort. They were my best friends in the world.

"So, where are you taking me? Is this another of your interventions? I'm not going to walk into a room full of friends and family again, am I?"

Kristine laughed. "Not this time. It's just us having an enjoyable meal out as friends."

"It's called Casa del Diablo. My friend, Russell, owns it," Sam added.

"Isn't that something to do with the devil?" Things were getting a little weird.

Death. Resurrection. Devils.

"It means House of the Devil. He says his food is so sinful the devil deserves to eat it." She laughed. "The food is exceptional, though."

The scenery flew by as we drove further out into the country, and I remember coming out this way with Kieran not long after he was diagnosed. Why did everything remind me of him?

Lost in my thoughts, it surprised me when we pulled into the car park and Kristine opened the door.

"You okay there, Jason?" She looked concerned, and I was so sorry to be the cause of her concern yet again.

"I'm good, and I'm starving."

A man I assumed was Russell greeted us as we entered the restaurant. It was a beautiful place, artfully decorated in reds and blacks but it didn't at all feel depressing. It created just the right ambience, and I was actually feeling quite excited to be out for a change.

That was until I saw the unmistakable figure of Mal. The man from the funeral parlour.

Shit.

"Everything okay?" Sam asked. "We can go if it's too much for you?"

"It's all good," I said and took her hand as Russell showed us to our table.

Fortunately, we were on the other side of the restaurant and with a little luck, he wouldn't see us and we could enjoy our evening. I didn't even know why I was so bothered by his presence. I didn't really know him, but I'd told him things about me and Kieran. Plus, he knew my intention.

I sat with my back to him, determined to ignore him and have a good night. Kristine and Sam discussed names for the baby. They held hands as they talked, and I envied them and their love for each other and the unborn baby Sam carried.

The food itself was excellent, and Russell himself came over several times to make sure we were enjoying ourselves.

I didn't miss the looks he gave me, and I wondered for a moment if this had been a setup, that maybe Kristine or Sam, or both of them, had arranged the whole thing. Kind of like a blind date, but not quite.

He was very attentive, placing his hand on my shoulder as he filled my wine glass for the third, or maybe it was the fourth, time. As much as I was flattered that someone was interested in me, I wasn't ready to return his attention.

The conversation at the table faltered, and a voice spoke.

"Jason. How nice to see you again." It washed over me, soothing me from the inside. Where Russell's attentiveness had made me fidgety, Mal's proximity warmed and reassured me.

Where the fuck had that come from?

I turned to face him and was momentarily lost for words. Gone was the suit, replaced by a more casual look: dark jeans teamed with a long-sleeved button-up shirt in lavender. A tantalising patch of hair peeked out.

Finally finding my voice, I spoke.

"Mal, fancy seeing you here."

He looked…good!

His dark, wavy hair was styled to perfection. He sported a

few days' old scruff on his face, and his warm, chocolate-brown eyes seemed to peer deep inside of me.

I was a mess by comparison. Ill-fitting clothes and dark-rimmed, sunken eyes.

The scowl on Russell's face at Mal's appearance was both unmistakable and priceless.

"You know each other?" He turned to Mal, a tightness to his smile. I wasn't sure what was going on here, but I had no desire to be involved.

"We met earlier today. I just thought I'd come over and say hello." The tone of Mal's voice made me shiver. There was an underlying authority, and Russell's confidence slipped for a moment, a brief flit of panic crossing his face.

It was gone as quickly as it came, and I wondered if I'd imagined it.

Kristine spoke up, slicing through the tension simmering between them.

"I'm Kristine, Jason's best friend, and this is Sam, my partner. Would you like to join us, Mal? We're about to have dessert."

I kicked her under the table, and her smile brightened. No doubt she was envisioning her 'moving on' plan.

"I really wouldn't want to intrude."

"I'm sure he's got better things to do than sit listening to baby talk, *Kristine*." I emphasised her name and hoped she'd take the hint.

She smirked at me, eyes sparkling. She was enjoying this far too much.

"Actually, while I'd love to join you, I have to get home to the dog," Mal said. "Who knows what he'll get up to if he's left alone too long."

I didn't miss the smug smile on Russell's face, but he was getting no further with me than Mal was, regardless of what he thought.

"Jason, Zeke will be in touch. Ladies, it was a pleasure to

meet you, but I'll bid you a very good evening. I'm sure Russell here will take care of you." There was a commanding tone to his voice again, and Russell nodded emphatically.

"I definitely will."

"Well, I'm sorry you couldn't stay. Maybe we'll see you again." Kristine deserved another kick for that comment, but I refrained. I'd be having words with her later.

All eyes were on him as he walked back to his own table.

"Where have you been hiding him?" Sam asked, taking as much pleasure in my discomfort as Kristine was.

"I met him today." I didn't say where. That was a can of worms I was unwilling to open right now.

"He's very good-looking," Kristine said. "Annnd he seemed very interested."

I shook my head. Whatever was going on with him was purely business, nothing more.

"He's bad news," Russell added. "Lives at the big place not far from here with his brother. I've heard things."

"What kind of things?" Kristine patted the chair next to her. "Tell us everything."

He sat, eager to talk about the man that had just left.

"Well, it's just a rumour, but I heard they have wild orgies at that place." He looked around, checking who was listening. "Mrs Gold, that's their housekeeper. She has to clean up all manner of messes at that place."

"How do you know this? Did Mrs Gold tell you?" Kristine asked, her eyes wide with interest.

"Not exactly, no."

"So it is just idle gossip. You've no hard evidence," she pushed.

Russell looked sheepish, caught out in a lie, perhaps?

"Anyway…" His face reddened as he stood. "I'll go grab your desserts. Won't be long."

He rushed away from the table, and we burst out laughing. It had been so long, and it felt good.

"I think someone didn't like Mal's arrival," Sam said, enjoying it far too much. "I think *someone* quite liked our Jason, though."

"No. No one quite liked 'our Jason'," I insisted. It was as ridiculous as it sounded.

A movement in my periphery had me glancing over to the door where Mal was about to leave. The heart I thought was all but dead fluttered as he smiled. Nothing huge, just a small lift of his lips, but something stirred in my chest. Was that excitement?

I dismissed the thought immediately. I'd just met the man, and I was in mourning. Grief took hold again, and I turned away, ignoring him.

Kieran was what mattered, not some tall, dark, brooding, handsome man I'd just met.

Kristine and Sam chattered away, and I retreated into myself as I usually did. I didn't deserve happiness or anyone else's love, and after dessert was done and Sam drove me home, I let myself into my gloomy house, grabbing a bottle of whisky and a glass from the cabinet.

Laughing tonight had felt so right, but here I was, betraying Kieran's memory by enjoying myself. Not only that, but I'd looked at a man in a way a grieving widower should never do. With interest.

It'd only been eighteen months. I didn't need to move on, I needed to get him back, and Zeke was going to help me.

CHAPTER
FIVE
MAL

The drive home took far longer than I wanted. My inner demon screamed at me for release. When was the last time that had happened? It was usually more than content to simmer inside of me, so twice in one day was unheard of, even in the other realm.

I pulled up to the house and ran inside, stripping off as I went. Mrs Gold had already gone home, so there was no danger of being discovered.

"Not now, Smokey," I shouted as he ran towards me, and, as if sensing my predicament, he growled, bared his huge teeth and followed me through the house.

He knew what came next.

I burst out of the back door and released my wings. Wind rushed through my hair as I took flight, dipping and swooping through the trees, twisting this way and that.

The relief as my demon broke free was immense.

Built for speed rather than aesthetics, my wings carried me swiftly out to the lake on the grounds of the house. I skimmed across the water, seeing my reflection in the mirror-like surface. I dipped my fingers in the water, watching as the ripples spread across it. Smokey sped along the shoreline, keeping pace. He loved to run as much as I loved to fly.

I rose higher, careful not to breach the canopy of trees. The last thing I needed was to be spotted. Zeke and I had worked so hard to appear as normal as we could. A winged beast flying over our estate would only fuel the speculation already held by the village.

I stifled the urge to whoop. Sound carried, but Smokey had no such compulsion and let rip with a blood-curdling howl.

"Quiet." I sent the command through the mind link we shared, and although he couldn't speak, he understood.

I left him and the estate behind, flying low over the farmers' fields, the wheat rustling as I soared above it. The village was close, and I dared not venture further for fear of being seen.

Feeling much better, I turned and headed for home. My demon was appeased for the moment, but I could tell it wouldn't be long before he demanded to be let loose again. Suspicious as to the reasons for his insistence to appear twice in one day, I decided to head to the library.

I landed at the rear door and collected my clothes as I walked back through the house. Smokey ran to his water bowl and drank greedily, water slopping everywhere, soaking the floor.

"I should make you clean that up," I told him.

He tilted his head as if listening, then bounded to his bed and collapsed. He was so unfit for a hellhound!

I chucked on my jeans and grabbed a beer from the fridge. Barefoot and bare-chested, I walked to the library.

Zeke was just coming through the front door, a flirty girl on each arm. Damn good job they hadn't arrived five minutes earlier, else they'd have seen more than they should have. At least Zeke could have wiped their memory, but that wasn't the point. It didn't work on everyone.

"Mal, meet Mercedes and Chelsea."

I rolled my eyes as they giggled. One reason I disliked humans.

"Have fun," I said. Footsteps sounded as they climbed the stairs, and I closed the library door. I did not need to hear his sexual antics this evening.

Grabbing an enormous volume from one shelf, I pored over the pages, searching for the information I wanted. It wasn't unusual for some demons to appear more than once a day. In fact, some of us spent more time in our demon form than as humans.

It was just unusual for me. I'd never experienced it before, only succumbing to my demon as an absolute necessity when he demanded release.

I flicked through the fragile pages. The volume was centuries old, owned by the family for years. We always kept it here in this realm. Things had a habit of disappearing otherwise.

Failing to find anything worthwhile, I called the only person who could help me…Dad.

"Son? To what do I owe this pleasure? We're not due to talk again until next week."

That was Dad, all business.

"I have a question about my demon."

"You mean the one you've had forever? Son, if you don't know how it works by now. Well, I don't know what to tell you."

"I know how it works." Well, I thought I did.

"So, why the call?"

I contemplated hanging up and telling him nothing, but I'd made the call now and he'd badger me until I told him.

"He's demanded release twice today. I know that's not unusual for you or Mum or even Zeke…"

"But for you, it's pretty much unheard of," he finished my sentence.

"Yes. I'm not used to it, and this last time, it was almost as if he couldn't wait. I almost didn't make it home in time."

"Mmmm, that's strange for you. It's usually only when a mate is near that something like that happens. I remember when I met your mother. Mine wanted out all the time, as did hers."

"Why didn't I know this? Surely this is Demon 101 information," I asked.

"Usually it is," he said, "but you've never really been interested in that side of things. I don't ever remember you having a mate or seeing you with anyone. It's always been strictly business with you."

"I don't like humans, you know this."

"But you've never had much contact with demons either, other than family members."

"My choice. I dislike them as much as I loathe humans." Only one demon had ever attracted my attention, and he was no longer around to do that.

"Only one thing springs to mind, and that's the possibility that a potential mate was near."

"What the fuck, Dad? That's ridiculous." I almost dropped the phone.

"Now, calm down. I could be wrong, but previous experiences suggest that to be the case. Have you encountered someone new? Someone you've not had contact with before?"

"Maybe. A human man." I spat the words out, not believing what I was hearing. Man or woman, demons weren't fussy, but it could only be Jason based on my demon's behaviour.

"Then go see *him* again. You'll only know when that happens. Unless, of course, you don't want it, in which case, avoid him like the plague."

Did I want to see him again? If Zeke went ahead with the deal, there was every chance I'd bump into him again. And what if he went ahead with the resurrection? Where would that leave me then?

A demon with no outlet was a dangerous thing. I'd need to go to the other realm, another place I detested.

At least here I could breathe, not be stifled by the family.

"What happens if nothing comes of a mating? What happens to my demon?"

"Ah, well. That can be tricky. I've seen some go on a killing spree, even slaughtering the intended mate. Other times they've committed suicide, and sometimes they fuck it out of their systems."

So anything then. That was no help at all.

"Son, I have to go. I've a meeting with the Boss shortly, and as much as I want to give you more information, I don't have an awful lot to go on. You know how he gets if I'm late."

"Yeah, I do. I'll see you in a day or so. I have a meeting in the realm too. I'll see you then." I bade him goodbye and ended the call.

He'd given me food for thought, a lot to think about. How I handled this information was down to me.

How the hell was Jason my mate? How, in all my years, had I never met one before? Why now?

So many questions, so few answers. Never had I experienced anything like this before. My demon had always been more than happy to sit undisturbed, for the most part, only wanting to be released when he'd been cooped up for too long.

Bael had been the only other one to have any kind of effect on him, but that had been nothing compared to what I was feeling now.

Talk about cluelessness. You'd think I'd know about these things, but I'd never had any interest. It was difficult to imagine I'd had so little contact with my own kind or humans, but that's how it was. To now think I could be mated to a human had my heart racing.

I cradled a glass of whisky in my hands as I sat at my desk. What a clusterfuck this was turning out to be.

All these years, avoiding demons and humans alike, then he walks in, nice as you like, waking the beast.

Fuck me!

I checked the time, surprised to see it was almost midnight.

We had a funeral tomorrow, and I couldn't afford to be late. I just hope Zeke remembered.

I knocked back the last of the whisky, grimacing at the burn. It was damn good stuff, and I had a barrel of it in the cellar, obtained a good few years ago from a distiller in Scotland. Now I thought about it, I was sure it was payment for a resurrection.

There were so many pitfalls associated with one, and I wasn't sure Jason had thought it through properly.

For a start, he'd have to move away from his friends and family. There was no way to explain it otherwise. The cost of a resurrection included the cost of new paperwork for both parties, and thanks to Yanni, we were now able to get these at a cheaper price.

Was he really prepared to give all that up? Especially seeing how his closest friend and her partner were about to have a baby. He'd miss that for sure.

Zeke would need to explain all this to him when they next met up. I was going to make sure I was far away from him when that happened. I wasn't about to risk running into him again with all this 'mate' business.

I'd move back to the other realm if that's what it took.

Clearly my demon was unhappy with this train of thought, and the buzz to release became an incessant itch.

Calm the fuck down, Mal. This is nothing you can't deal with, I told myself.

I hoped this pep talk would work. I really didn't want to go out again, especially as it had started to rain.

I could almost hear my inner demon grumbling. I didn't care. It was time for bed.

The wild noises coming from Zeke's room were unmistakable. No doubt he was having a good time, but I banged on the door anyway. It might have been petty, but at least one of us needed a good night's sleep.

Fortunately, I was at the other end of the house. Bounding feet announced Smokey's arrival. Despite having his own place to sleep downstairs, he preferred my room. It was no hardship, except for the snoring.

Always the snoring!

Unable to sleep, I lay awake running over the events of the day, from my first meeting with Jason to seeing him at the restaurant and the reappearance of my demon.

His grief was so close to the surface you'd think his husband had died weeks ago, not eighteen months. I'd spotted him the moment he'd walked into the restaurant with his friends, watched him laugh with them, but I'd also seen him get lost in himself as they talked amongst themselves.

His wistful stares at the couples around him were a dead giveaway. He tried so hard to hide it, smile when he needed to, but the telltale signs were there.

My demon wasn't exactly happy when the owner of the restaurant turned up and started to lay his hands on Jason. At first, I'd thought he was being nice, but the more he did it, the more I realised he was flirting with him.

I hadn't intended on going over to them, but my demon was insistent, and now I understood a little more why. If, and this was a big fucking if. If he was my mate, the attention of another man wouldn't have been tolerated.

It was all so obvious now.

What the hell was I going to do with this information? How could I be mated to a human? This was the question running on repeat through my mind. The easiest and best answer was that I wasn't, that this was all some stupid mistake.

An anomaly with my demon, it had to be that.

I'd call Dad again, see if he had any more advice. I couldn't tell Zeke. He'd tease me relentlessly. I had to keep it a secret from him.

Luckily, we'd be busy for the next couple of days. A couple of funerals and a planned visit to the other realm. Seemed like a good time to do a little more digging. Zeke would be in charge of the business, and I didn't know if that was a blessing or a curse.

You'd think Smokey's loud snores would keep me awake, but they were strangely soothing and before long, I slept.

My dreams were filled with a thin man whose eyes said more than words ever could, and I woke the next morning feeling like I hadn't slept.

Mrs Gold was already in the kitchen when I arrived, a smiling Zeke sitting on a stool at the breakfast bar.

"You look like shit!" he said, laughing.

"Ezekiel. Watch your language." Mrs Gold cuffed him around the ear before looking at me. "You do look terrible, though, Malcolm."

"I didn't sleep well. Someone kept me up all night," I said, glaring at Zeke.

"Well, one of us has to have a good time. Might as well be me."

"I'm going on a business trip tomorrow. Make sure you take care of what we discussed while I'm gone. Mrs Gold, take the next couple of days off. Zeke here can look after himself."

"Of course, dearie. Sit down and eat your breakfast. Sounds like you have a busy few days coming up."

I definitely did. I just hoped Zeke was able to conclude the business while I was away.

CHAPTER
SIX

JASON

Two days had passed, and I still hadn't heard from Zeke. On edge didn't even begin to cover how I felt. I'd snapped at Kristine so many times. It was a wonder she was still here.

The atmosphere in the shop was close to combusting, and I was trying my hardest to stay out of her way. Conversations were limited to one-word answers, and I knew I had to do something to salvage the downturn in our relationship. Either make up with her or contact Zeke. Neither was my preferred option.

"Coffee," she said, slamming a mug on my desk and spilling the hot liquid over the papers I was working on. In my effort to clear the pool of spreading coffee, I swiped at it and knocked the mug to the floor. It was then I noticed the mug.

It was Kieran's.

She gasped and looked at me, her eyes filling with tears.

"I am so sorry, Jason. I didn't think."

I could have shouted at her; the urge was there, but it was no one's fault.

"It's fine. Don't worry about it," I said, bending down to collect the broken shards from the floor.

She stifled a sob and ran from the office. Things were

going from bad to worse, and I knew there and then, something had to be done. Not just with Zeke, but I wouldn't lose Kristine over something so petty. It was just a mug, except it wasn't.

Seeing the shattered mug brought a fresh wave of sadness. Piece by piece he was disappearing from my life.

After clearing up the mess, I went back out into the shop. Kristine was sitting behind the counter, her puffy, red eyes and tear-stained face making me feel like a right dick.

"I'm sorry." I stood with my hands in my pockets, hoping she'd forgive my childish behaviour these past few days.

"I'm sorry too. I didn't even realise it was his mug until it smashed. Can you forgive me?" A fresh bout of tears started, and I rushed to her side, taking both her hands in mine.

"It's all forgiven. I'm the one that should be sorry, over and over. I've been an absolute arsehole to you, and you've been nothing but kind since, you know." I still found it difficult to utter the words.

"Can we be friends again?" How could I resist her plea? This was all my fault.

"We were never not friends. I just had a stupid mood on me the past few days."

"Yeah, you can be a twat sometimes." That brought a small smile to her face, and I knew we'd be ok.

"Hey, you can't call your boss that," I joked and handed her another tissue. She wiped her eyes, smudging her mascara.

"You might want to…" I motioned to her eyes and grabbed a mirror from one of the tables.

"Oh my God!" She jumped up from her chair and ran to the bathroom, leaving me laughing in her wake.

At least we were back on speaking terms, albeit fragile.

My phone buzzed with a message, and Zeke's number flashed up on the screen.

Shit!

It was now or never. I refused to lose any more of myself or him to his futile death.

> Meet me at the FP in an hour. I have news for you. Z

My heart rate kicked up a notch as panic surged through my body. Was I doing the right thing?

When Kristine walked back into the shop, she looked much better. Her make-up had been reapplied, but she still had the telltale flush of someone who had been crying.

"Let's close up early today. There's not much happening, and I think we could both do with a break, don't you?"

Relief washed over her, and she smiled gratefully. "It'd be nice to spend some time with Sam. She's working from home today."

"Then go be with her. I'll close up and call you later, make sure you are ok."

I closed up the shop, locked the door, and retreated to my office. It was preferable to going home where I'd mope around the house. There'd been times I found myself looking at Kieran's ashes. I'd not yet had time to scatter or bury them.

He'd had little to no family other than a brother and me. His parents had died some years earlier. He'd been an only child. They'd had him quite late in life, and illness had also taken them before their time. I hadn't known them, but my family had loved him as their own, as devastated as I was with his passing.

I pulled out my phone and read the message again.

Bringing him back to life was a huge step, and the logistics of it weren't lost on me. The biggest hurdle was how I'd explain it to everyone.

Would Zeke alter their minds? The more I thought about it, the more complex the problem until there was only one thing to do.

"Hi, Zeke, it's Jason."

"Ah, my man. Sorry I didn't get back to you earlier. Business, you know? Can you come by later? Mal and I need to go through a few things with you. Contracts and such like."

Wow, I hadn't given that any thought and presumed they'd just do it under the table, so to speak.

"I can do that. Is now too soon?"

"Nope, now's great. See you then."

It was now or never.

Zeke greeted me at Perfect Shores, but there was no sign of Mal. Slightly disappointed, I followed Zeke to a small room, complete with comfortable chairs and flowers. From the surroundings, I gathered this was a room set aside for grieving families.

Papers and a pen were set on the small table in the middle of the room, and realisation set in that I was actually going to do this.

I wiped my hands down my trousers and took a seat. Zeke sat on the other side and leant forward, his arms resting on his thighs.

"I know Mal didn't get a chance to go through it all with you. So, that's what we'll do today. I've drawn up contracts, and if you're completely sure this is what you want to do, we can get them signed and begin the process. If you're unsure, you can take them away, have a read and get back to me."

I nodded. "I understand."

"Right then. Let me explain how this will work. First question, how long has your loved one been dead? Eighteen months?"

I nodded again, my words sticking in my throat.

"We're pushing the boundaries there. We try not to go too long after death. Twelve months is the optimum. Anything after that and things can get a little 'messy', shall we say."

I didn't know what he meant by that, and I wasn't sure I wanted to know.

"The process is fairly simple. We'll need something of his, your written consent and £50,000. This covers the actual resurrection, including paperwork for your disappearance."

I looked at him wide-eyed. Disappearance? £50,000?

"I, er. What do you mean? Disappearance."

Zeke laughed. "Did you honestly think you'd be able to stick around after bringing him back? What would your friends and loved ones think? Assuming you have them."

"I do, yes. I just thought…"

"Not many consider the repercussions of bringing the dead back to life. What were you expecting?"

I sat back in the chair, stunned.

I had visions of selling my soul to the devil, minds being wiped clean, and Kieran being accepted as alive again.

How fucking naive had I been?

"Seems more like a business deal."

"That's exactly what it is. Death is our business. We bury the bodies and reap the souls. Well, except when we resurrect them." He laughed again. "Gotta love that motto."

My indecision must have been evident. I bit my lip, the metallic taste of blood on my tongue. It was a nervous habit.

"Not what you were expecting, eh? The reality of it rarely is." Zeke, too, sat back in his chair and steepled his fingers. "Maybe you should go away and decide if this is what you really want. It's a lot to take in and a big decision, considering this is only a short-term situation."

Now he really had my attention.

"What do you mean? Short term? Maybe you should have led with that."

"I thought Mal had gone through all this with you? Let me go grab him."

Before I could protest, Zeke was up and out the door. I picked up a contract from the table and skimmed the first few lines. It read like any other contract I'd seen: a place for names to be inserted and a list of terms and conditions.

They were exactly as he'd said, but when I got to the part about renewed life, the length of it made me question my decision to do this.

Twelve months. That was all. Twelve short months. But it'd be a year where he'd be well.

We'd be able to take the holiday in paradise we'd planned. I'd have him to myself. No work, no one else. Just me and him.

I felt my earlier uncertainty start to wane. I could explain it away to Kristine and Sam. My family would understand if I told them I needed to get away from it all.

It was doable, and the more I thought about it, the more my mind was made up. A year would give me time to get used to being without him again. We could spend the time doing all the things we wanted to before he died.

The door opened, and in walked Mal, closely followed by Zeke.

Before either one could speak, I stood, determined to say my piece.

"I'll do it," I blurted out. "Where do I sign?"

"Great, I'll get you the pen." Zeke reached around me and snatched it from the table.

"Wait!" Mal's stern voice stopped us both in our tracks. "Have you really thought this through?"

"What are you doing, Mal?" Zeke asked, a frown on his face. "Jason has made up his mind."

"I have. It's what I want," I told him.

Why was he so bothered? It was fifty grand in their pocket. This was my decision.

He opened his mouth to speak again but instead walked from the room, slamming the door behind him.

"I'm sorry about that, Jason. If you just want to sign here and here." Zeke indicated two crosses on the paper and handed me the pen. "You do understand, once you've signed, there is no going back. It's a binding contract. Not legally, but you will be bound by other conditions. Perhaps you should read those before you sign."

"What do you mean? I thought it was just cash."

"Eh, technically, yes. There might be a small blood deposit too."

I gulped. I hated needles after seeing Kieran in the hospital, and I told Zeke as much.

"No needles involved. Don't worry about that. We just slice your palm with a knife, drip some into a bowl and that's it! Bob's your uncle, Fanny's your aunt."

He said it so matter-of-fact, as if I was of no consequence. "And what happens to the blood?"

"So, are you still signing? Bank details are right there." He tapped the page with the end of the pen.

"I'll sign it, Zeke. Having Kieran back is the most important thing to me. If I have to disappear, then I'll do that." I just hoped Kieran thought it was the right thing when he came back, although why wouldn't he?

"Once we have the funds, I'll be in touch. If you can just get me something with his DNA, then we can start the process. I suggest you start making plans to disappear. It can take time. Pictures of him and you would be good so we can arrange the relevant paperwork."

I guess I thought the process would be more supernatural, more akin to voodoo, than this apparent business transaction. I had no idea what they did on their end, but I'd been expecting pentagrams, spells and lots of chanting.

Instead, I'd got a contract and a considerably lighter bank balance.

My hand hovered over the page. Was it the right thing? The ache in my heart told me it was. The thought of seeing his brilliant smile, feeling his arms around me as we made love, his warmth, laughter. Imagining a life without him was unbearable, and even though it wouldn't be forever, in my eyes, the sacrifice was worth it.

I signed my name with a flourish. It felt so very right…or did it? An uncomfortable sense of dread filled my chest. The lightness I'd felt in my heart, disappeared, replaced by an impending feeling of doom.

"Are you ok?" Zeke asked.

"Yeah, I'm ok, I think. A little bit of discomfort in my chest is all."

"Ah, that can happen. Once the contract is signed, most of our clients describe a lightness, a feeling of peace and tranquillity."

Well, fuck. I wasn't feeling any of that, and my face must have reflected it.

"You're not feeling that?" he asked, a worried look on his face.

I shook my head. "No. Is that bad?"

He took a second to answer. "Not always. Sometimes it's just because there was some indecision in you. It's probably nothing to worry about."

Why didn't I feel appeased by his statement? Why didn't I believe him? But as the tension in my chest eased slightly, I again convinced myself it was the right thing to do.

"I'll transfer the money once I'm back at the shop." Fortunately, Kieran's life insurance money would more than cover the fee they were asking. "I'll have the other things ready for you in a day or two. What about the blood thing?"

"When you hand everything over, that's when we'll do it," Zeke said.

I laughed. "I thought I'd be selling the devil my soul."

He laughed too, a little nervously. "Who says you aren't?"

"You said—" I couldn't even complete my sentence.

"I'm just messing with you, man. Quit worrying." He shuffled with the papers on the table and stood, his hand outstretched.

I shook it and followed him out of the room.

The hairs on my neck stood on end as I reached the front door. Instinctively, I turned to see Mal watching me from the door to his office.

He didn't look happy. What the hell business was it of his? It was my life.

Before I could do or say anything, he retreated and closed the door.

Why did I think I'd just signed my life away, and why did I get the feeling this wasn't going to end well?

CHAPTER
SEVEN

MAL

After watching Jason leave, my demon wasn't happy, fighting for release. I removed my jacket and tie, trying to ease some of the pressure building inside my body.

"What the fuck were you thinking?" Zeke shouted as he exploded through the door, almost knocking it off its hinges.

"It's not right. This one has a wrongness about it, and you know it too." I squared up to him, my demon growing in stature, dwarfing him.

Zeke wasn't intimidated at all and challenged me, toe to toe.

"What is your fucking issue with this one? From the moment you first met him, you've been telling me not to go ahead with it."

"I can't explain it," I shouted. The demon inside knew exactly what was going on, but there was no way I could explain that to Zeke. He'd laugh in my face.

"Try, for fuck's sake. It's fifty grand easy money, Mal."

"We don't need the money, and we don't need to do this one. We're already cutting it close. Twelve months is usually the max. His husband has been gone eighteen. What if it doesn't work?"

Zeke walked over to the window overlooking our Garden of Serenity.

"I don't get it. You *never* get this involved with a resurrection. There's something you're not telling me, and I *will* find out. He's signed the contract anyway, so there's fuck all you can do. He's transferring the money later."

"Cancel it."

"You know I can't do that. Once they sign, it's begun. The money comes next, and once the bleeding happens, you know it's a done deal."

"If you don't call it off, I will." I took a step towards him; he needed to stop this.

"You know what? Fuck you, Mal, but you're playing with fire."

"I'm used to it. Nothing I haven't dealt with before. I'm going to go see him, tell him we can't do it. I have the authority in this business, not you."

"You'll make me look stupid. I offered him the opportunity, and you're just going to go ahead and call it off. Well, thanks for that. I wish I knew what was going on inside of your head. You've been acting strange these past few days. Do whatever the fuck you want."

He stormed out again and slammed the door. It wasn't the first time he'd done this, and it wouldn't be the last. We clashed more than we got on.

This was wrong, though. I could feel it.

While in the other realm, I'd sought advice on near-date resurrections, and it confirmed what I suspected. It could all go horribly wrong, and the consequences for them both could be dire.

Kieran might come back incomplete, and Jason could die. It was as simple as that. I wouldn't usually care, but he was different, and if what my father had told me was true, he was my mate.

I didn't want to contemplate what my demon would or could do should he die. I had to at least try to talk him out of it.

THE DOORBELL RANG as I entered All That Glitters. I was greeted by a very surprised Kristine.

"Mal, how lovely to see you again. Did you want Jason? He's just in his office."

"If he's about."

"I'll go tell him you're here."

I browsed the tables laden with knick-knacks and picked up a few that interested me. Most were inexpensive pieces you'd find in most antique stores, but a few, held in the locked cabinets, would fetch a pretty penny at auction.

"Mal. What are you doing here?" Jason looked pissed, and I couldn't blame him.

"I just wanted to talk to you. Could we go somewhere private?"

"I've nothing to say to you. My mind's made up." He pouted.

"I'm just going to go out back. Leave you two to talk." I watched as Kristine quietly left, leaving us alone.

"I don't think Zeke explained everything to you. This could be dangerous…for both of you."

"Why are you so bothered, Mal?"

Good fucking question. How did I explain my reasons to him?

Before we could talk any further, the bell rang and the door opened again.

"Ah, Brendan. I was so sorry to hear about your mother." Jason approached the man who had entered.

The guy standing at the door was good-looking, suave and well-dressed. I'd seen the likes of him before.

"Thank you, Jason. Your sincerity is touching." I bristled as he touched Jason's arm. His familiarity had my demon panting, ready to pounce.

An involuntary growl built in my throat, and they both looked my way.

"Mal? Is everything alright?" Jason asked.

I nodded, unable to speak.

"I'm sorry, Jason. Were you in the middle of something? I can come back, or maybe we could go out for a coffee or dinner. I wanted to talk to you about some of my mother's things. She wanted you to have them, and so do I."

Again with the touching, and by now, my demon was going ballistic. Ready to tear this piece of shit limb from limb. No one touched Jason.

"Let me get my diary, and we'll pencil something in." He went out back to his office, leaving me with Brendan.

"Who are you?" I asked, walking over to him.

"A good friend of Jason's. Why do you ask?"

"No reason. What's your interest in him?" Was he a boyfriend, a lover? My demon needed to know.

I stepped away from him as Jason walked back in.

"I could do it tomorrow at three. I'll meet you at the coffee shop just down from here. You know the one?"

Brendan nodded and leant in for a hug. A fucking hug!

"Take your hands off him." I couldn't have stopped the words if I'd wanted to, and by now, my demon was ready to rip Brendan's head off.

I took a step forward, and they broke apart.

"What the hell is wrong with you, Mal?" Jason asked.

"Is he a friend of yours?" I asked him. I was not making this any better.

"What he is is the son of a very good customer of mine, and I'll thank you to leave."

This was not going to plan. "We still need to talk, Jason," I insisted.

"It's ok. I'm going." Brendan headed towards the door. "I'll see you tomorrow, Jason. I'm really looking forward to it."

He was goading me, and as Jason placed the book on the counter, he flashed a brilliant smile, all teeth and smugness.

"You'd best fucking explain what's going on here, Mal, before I call the police and report you for harassment," Jason said once we were alone.

"Can we take this somewhere else? I need to explain."

"Kristine," he shouted. "I'm just going out with Mal. I'll be back in five minutes."

"Of course." She was so close to the door; I wondered what she'd heard. A good job I hadn't discussed the resurrection with Jason.

"The resurrection might not work," I told him as we sat in a corner of the coffee shop. He'd said hello to the young barista as we entered, and I got the feeling he came here often.

"What do you mean? Zeke said it would work." He'd calmed down a little and was at least willing to listen.

"Zeke didn't tell you everything. We're really close to the cut-off point for performing this, and the chances of it working are minimal. If he does come back, there's every chance he might not be the Kieran you know. Add the fact that once you go through the 'bleeding', you too could be compromised. You could also die."

I was to the point. Matter-of-fact. No point in sugar-coating things or wrapping them up in a pretty bow. He could lose his life.

"I need him back. You don't understand." Droplets of coffee spilt on the table as his hands shook.

"No, I don't. You're absolutely right, but think of what you could be losing." What the hell was I saying?

"But I'd have my Kieran back."

"You would, but you'd not see Kristine and Sam go through the best possible time of their life. They will need you."

I was pulling out all the stops here, trying to get him to change his mind.

I could see he was wavering as I knew he would when I mentioned them.

"How long would it be before you saw the baby?" I continued. "That's assuming you live through the resurrection. Do you think they'd understand?"

He sat back in his chair, a resigned look on his face.

"Did you feel the rush of euphoria when you signed the contract? The surge of adrenaline? The feeling of peace?" I pushed.

I couldn't know for certain, but from the look on his face, I didn't think he had. That was always a strong indicator that things wouldn't go well. Zeke should have known that and told Jason. I was going to fucking kill him.

Sometimes the money was all-important to him. He was a materialistic bastard. I knew how that sounded with me driving the Aston, but that was different. I didn't flaunt our wealth, which was more than I could say for Zeke.

"I didn't, no." He bit his lip, worry etched on his face. A bead of blood formed on his lip, and it was all I could do not to swipe it away. I gripped my coffee mug tight, resisting the urge.

"You know it's not right, Jason." I spoke quietly, letting him know I understood.

The face that looked back at me was distraught, eyes brimming with unshed tears, and I saw the realisation hit that bringing Kieran back was the wrong thing to do.

"You're not a stupid man, Jason. Grief makes us do irrational things. I know you want him back, but live with your memories of him, keep them close in your heart. Don't lose yourself to it. You'll lose everyone you love that way and be left with nothing."

"I already signed the contract. There's no going back." His voice wavered.

"If you really want out, I can help you with that." I wasn't sure I could, but I'd try.

The more we talked about cancelling this, the happier my demon became.

"Can you give me some time?" He asked.

"I can, but I don't think you need it. You know in your heart this is the right thing. Think of Kristine, Sam and their unborn child. I know you still love Kieran, but this isn't the right way to remember him, Jason."

Getting him out of the contract would mean another trip to the other realm. Twice in as many days was unheard of for me, but I was willing to do what it took to release him from the deal. We all knew it was wrong, me and Zeke included.

Now my only problem was what to do about the mating situation. That could wait. One step at a time. If I could get Jason on my side, then there was a chance.

Why on earth I was even considering this was beyond me. I hated humans almost as much as I hated demons, and here I was, helping out a human with a view to making him my mate.

A grieving human at that.

"What are you?"

Jason's question startled me. I'd never been asked that before. There'd never been any reason for anyone *to* ask me.

"I don't know what you mean. I'm a human, same as you."

"I know you're not. You said it yourself, I'm not a stupid man. Humans don't resurrect the dead."

He had me there. Nothing was written that we couldn't divulge what we were, but there was an unspoken rule. Unless it was absolutely necessary, we kept the secret to ourselves, but in this instance, I felt compelled to tell him.

"We're demons."

"And you run a funeral parlour." It was a statement more than a question.

"We do."

"And you resurrect the dead."

"Only if the circumstances are right." I'd usually refuse to answer, but for Jason, I was making an exception.

He laughed out loud, turning a few heads.

"What's so funny?" I began to laugh too, his laughter infectious.

"I don't really know. These past few days have been a whirlwind for me. I got a haircut, where I met your brother, considered bringing my dead husband back to life and met a demon. Who'd have fucking thought it? Oh and I've been hit on by two guys I have no interest in whatsoever."

Well, that was good news. Unless one of them was me.

"And who might that be?"

"Brendan and Russell. They're not my type."

It was on the tip of my tongue to ask what his type was, but my skills at talking to humans were limited. I certainly didn't know how to talk to someone I was interested in. He answered before I could open my mouth.

"I don't want to be hit on. I want to be treated like a person, not someone to be pitied because I lost my husband. I'm sure the night at the restaurant was a set-up, and Brendan? He's always been the same, even when Kieran was alive, always flirting."

"Perhaps *we* could meet up for coffee again? Just as friends. I'm not hitting on you, and I promise we won't talk about death. I actually have an interest in antiques."

He tilted his head and looked at me for a moment, hopefully coming to a favourable decision.

"Me, a human, going for coffee with a demon. I'm sure there's a joke in there somewhere, but as long as you're not going to hit on me, I think I can do that."

My demon preened, pleased with himself at his words.

"I'll call on you again, Jason, if that would be ok."

"That's very formal, Mal, but I think we could be friends. God knows I've not had many of those since I lost Kieran, and you did talk me out of making what could have been a very big mistake. I was blinded by the fact I could see him again. I didn't stop to think of the consequences."

"Not many do, and I'll be honest with you, most of the time, I don't care."

"Why me then? Why am I so different?"

I'd already given him enough information today. Telling him I thought he was my mate would be a step too far. I answered him the only way I could.

"I don't know. You just are."

The next ten minutes passed in silence as we both drank our coffee, glancing at each other over our mugs, a truce of sorts having been made, and when I left him at the door to his shop, he uttered one single word.

"Thanks."

The bell rang as he opened the door and slowly stepped inside.

That had to be one of the most bizarre afternoons I'd had in my very long life, but I'd do it all again to spend time with him.

A feeling I'd never felt before washed over me, the need to look after him, to protect him from the hurt only the death of a loved one could bring.

The need to make him my mate.

What the fuck was I going to do now?

CHAPTER
EIGHT

JASON

Y ou look different today," Kristine said as I walked into work the next day.

"What do you mean? Is it the haircut?" I fiddled with the strands, my fingers sticky from the product I'd put in it this morning. I'd actually made an effort today. I'd showered, shaved and was even wearing something resembling business attire.

"No, it's not that. You seem, I don't know how to explain it, lighter. Less stressed, I suppose. I can't quite put my finger on it." She handed me a cup of coffee, and we sat behind the counter. It was still early, both of us having come in to do a stock take.

I knew the reason for the change in my demeanour. Arriving home last night after making my decision, I'd headed straight for my old bedroom and stripped the bed, replacing it with a set of new covers I'd bought but never used.

I'd admit it was hard, and I'd cried for an hour, but it was cathartic in some way, releasing some of the pent-up emotional baggage I'd been carrying for a year. I still spent my night in my single bed, not yet ready to take that next step.

Talking with Mal yesterday had woken something inside of me, a long-forgotten feeling starting to spark, and while I still wasn't over Kieran, there was a light at the end of the tunnel.

I shrugged. "I was thinking about what you said about moving on."

"Really?" Her eyes lit up. "I know it's only been eighteen months, and believe me when I say that I know it's not easy to get over someone so quickly. I'm not telling you to go out and find the nearest man. Sam and I just want you back for us and for our baby. She deserves to know that her guncle is a fun-loving guy."

"Did you just say she?"

Her hand flew to her mouth. "Oh, shit. I wasn't supposed to tell anyone. Don't tell Sam you know. She'll kill me."

"What's it worth? I'm sure I can blackmail you for something. How about a bottle of that lovely wine we both love? You know, the *really* expensive one."

"You wouldn't tell her." She smacked my arm, and I had to laugh. "Would you?"

"I won't tell, I promise. Your secret is safe with me, but I'm so pleased it's a girl! That's brilliant news."

"I know. We're both really excited. We're planning out the nursery, and I bought her this." Kristine grabbed her phone and flicked through it, finally showing me the cutest little red-and-white gingham dress.

"That is adorable. I'm going to need to do some shopping for my little girl."

"Aw, that's so sweet to hear you say that." She leant forward and gave me an awkward side hug. "Uncle Jason, I like that."

"Me too, Kristine. Me too." I would have missed this, had I gone through with the 'resurrection' as they called it. Not just if I'd died, which was a snippet Zeke had failed to mention, but if it had been successful, I wouldn't have been here anyway.

I'd be somewhere on the other side of the world. Admittedly I'd be with Kieran, but Kristine needed me. I realised that now.

"Well, let's get this inventory logged and priced, then we can go out for dinner later. I fancy some devil's food again."

"Don't forget you're having coffee with Brendan later," she reminded me as she took the coffee cups into the kitchen.

I groaned, remembering how I'd made the appointment out of churlishness rather than because I wanted to go. Mal had totally rubbed me the wrong way, and his apparent dislike of Brendan had made me do the one thing I didn't really want to do —go for coffee with him!

"Ah, fuck. Can't you go? Make some excuse for me?"

"No, you made the appointment, and he might have some nice knick-knacks we can buy from him. His mother had some lovely jewellery. Come on, take one for the team."

There was taking one for the team, then there was walking into the lion's den.

"Fine, I suppose I'll go, but if I'm not back after half an hour, come get me."

Three o'clock came around far too quickly, and we were still only halfway through the stock take.

"I should cancel. We've still so much to do," I said to her as I locked the glass case. It could wait until tomorrow, but I was trying to put off my meeting with Brendan.

"It'll be fine. You'll be in the middle of a coffee shop. He's not going to do anything there."

"That man is incorrigible. He'd hit on his own brother if he thought he could gain something from it. He's only doing it to get a good price for the items."

I sighed dramatically, and Kristine laughed.

"Go, I'll come get you in half an hour," she said, pushing me out of the door.

The coffee shop was busy when I walked in. Maybe I'd be in luck and we wouldn't be able to find a seat, but then I saw him. He waved and stood as I approached the table, greeting me with a kiss on the cheek. What the actual fuck?

Flustered, I sat on the other side of the table from him, and he pushed a coffee towards me.

"I ordered for you. That lovely young man, Harry, told me what you usually drank. We drink the same, how funny? We've so much in common."

"So, what did you want to talk about? You said you had some things of your mother's you wanted to sell?" I didn't want to have anything in common with him at all.

"Well, ok then. Business first." He opened the bag he had with him and spread a handful of photographs on the table. The first was a picture of a gorgeous emerald necklace.

"You'd be better selling this to a specialist, Brendan. We don't usually deal with this type of thing." I picked up each photograph and looked closely. Each picture was of a valuable piece of jewellery. "We deal with lots of things, but nothing this good. I couldn't give you market value for these. Maybe one of the high-end auction houses would be better."

He didn't seem bothered at all and placed them back into his bag.

"Business is done. Now how about dinner later?"

"I think I've made it clear before, I'm not interested, Brendan."

"I just thought, now your husband is out of the picture, we could get together. There's nothing to keep us apart now."

"Whoa, you've read this all wrong. I'm just here to talk about your mother's things, not to start anything with you."

"Aw, come on. I could tell you were only holding back because your husband was there. We have a spark, don't you think?"

The man was delusional. The only spark I'd felt was when I shook hands with Mal. This conversation was over. I was about to tell him he was no longer welcome in the store when a hand gripped my wrist, hard.

"Let me go, Brendan. You're hurting me." I tried to pull away, but he held on tighter, pulling my chair closer to his.

"You want this as much as I do, Jason. I know you do."

His grip tightened as I struggled to get away. You'd think with the number of people in here, they'd see a man being assaulted, but as close as he sat to me, most would think we were lovers having a quiet cup of coffee.

Anger coursed through me. Why didn't anyone see this?

"Take your hands off him." Those same words as yesterday, spoken with the same authority.

Mal. Thank fuck for that.

"This has nothing to do with you," Brendan hissed.

"It has everything to do with me. Now step away from him and get the hell out of here."

I only had eyes for the giant of a man standing next to me, his eyes flashing with barely concealed rage.

"Do as he says, Brendan. I won't tell you again. There's nothing between us. I suggest you leave and don't come back to the shop again."

My heart was pounding in my chest as Brendan released me, snatched his bag from the floor and flounced out of the coffee shop.

That same shock of electricity passed between us as Mal touched my shoulder reassuringly.

"Are you ok?" he asked gently.

"Yeah, just a bit shook up." I looked down at the red finger marks on my wrist. They didn't really hurt, but I was pissed at being put in such a position.

"Here, let me look." Tingles spread through me as he took my arm and stroked the bruised skin.

I held my breath, the brush of his fingers delicate, setting my skin on fire.

"If you want me to kill him, I will. I could always use a soul or two." I wasn't sure if he was joking or not.

"A little dramatic, Mal," I said with a smile and moved my hand to my lap. His touch was causing all kinds of sensations, ones I hadn't felt in a very long time. "How come you're here? Did you enjoy the coffee so much yesterday?"

"Right place, right time. Or maybe I didn't trust him when I met him yesterday. Either way, it was a good job I was here. No telling what pricks like him will do."

"I'm not a damsel in distress, you know. You didn't have to ride in on your white horse to save me. I would have got rid of him."

"I know. Like I said, I was just in the right place at the right time. Now, how about we order some more coffee and talk about all the ways I can torture him before I kill him?"

As much as I would love to do that, I'd been gone from the shop long enough. "I should go, actually. I left Kristine in the middle of a stock take. How about, as a thank-you, you join us for dinner tonight? We're going to Casa del Diablo again."

"I don't know. I wouldn't want to intrude."

"You'd be most welcome. No doubt Kristine will want to hug you after your heroics today. Although maybe you should torture her too. She refused to take my place today."

"In that case, I'd love to join you. Shall I pick you up?"

That sounded an awful lot like a date. "We'll meet you there, if that's ok. I'm sure it's out of your way. Shall we say seven?"

"Perfect," he said, his voice akin to how I imagined warm chocolate would sound. It washed over me, deep and sensual, with a commanding tone. I'm sure the lovers he used it on would be putty in his hands. That would never be me. I'd vowed to stay true to Kieran for the rest of my life.

Except... No, except nothing. I was a grieving widower. A thankful one, but a widower all the same.

"Thanks again, Mal."

I followed him outside, the sun warm for a change. Heads turned as he put on his sunglasses and walked away confidently, his perfectly fitting trousers hugging his thick thighs.

Good Lord! What in God's name was wrong with me? I had

no right to be thinking about him like that, but he did have a nice arse too and I couldn't help but admire it.

The shop was empty of customers when I returned. Kristine was sitting cross-legged on the floor, counting teaspoons.

"Did you know, we have over one hundred of these? Why do we need that many?" she asked, holding one up for my inspection.

I sat down next to her, my legs outstretched and picked up one of the offending items. It wasn't special, just a plain teaspoon with a little pattern on the handle.

"I have absolutely no idea, but you know what, let's get rid of them." I stood and looked around the store. Tables full of bric-a-brac, cabinets full of everyone else's junk. I'd lost focus since Kieran had died, leaving most things to Kristine.

She'd done an amazing job, but her talent didn't lie with antiques, unfortunately.

"You can't just get rid of them, Jason." She looked shocked.

"Why not? Let's start afresh. We'll take the stuff we don't need to the auctions and keep the good stuff. We'll start a website and advertise the higher-end items. We should change the name too."

It was time for a change. I'd wallowed in pity for far too long. Was I ready to do this? Kieran would always be with me, there was no doubting that, but this needed to be done if I was to move on.

"How about Barr and Butler?" I held my hand out to her and helped her to her feet.

She pouted. "I like All That Glitters."

"I do too, but Barr and Butler sounds more professional. What do you think? Do you want to be my partner instead of just working here? Instead of just doing house clearances, we could branch out. Visit auction houses. I'm sure there's courses you could go on. Say yes, Kristine, please?"

I knelt down before her, my hands clenched in front of me.

"Hey, Casanova. Stop muscling in on my woman."

Trust Sam to choose that moment to walk into the store.

"He was begging me to become his partner," Kristine said.

"You know she's a lesbian, right? She has no interest in the thing dangling between your legs."

"Yeah, I know." I struggled to my feet, feeling every one of my thirty-five years.

"Kristine said we were going out later. We'll pick you up at about half six. I've booked a table for three with Russell."

"Any chance you could make it four?" In my eagerness to change the store around, I'd forgotten to mention Mal joining us for dinner.

"Oh, so the coffee date with Brendan went well." Kristine's smile was wide.

"Not exactly. He, erm, tried it on with me, and I was saved by a tall, dark, handsome man. I invited him for dinner as a thank-you."

"Does this man have a name? I'm so happy for you." Sam and Kristine squealed with barely disguised delight.

"It was Mal, ok? He came in as Brendan had a hold of my wrist." I held it out for them to see, the red now starting to fade to pink.

"I'll cut his balls off if he even walks past the door." I loved that Kristine was also angry on my behalf.

"What a complete twat," Sam added. "I bet that hot hunk of a man sent him away with his tail between his legs. Are you ok, sweetie?"

"I'm perfectly fine, but as a token of my appreciation, I invited him to dinner. So, you need to be on your best behaviour. No telling stories and no trying to set me up. We're just friends."

Little did I know that the night would not turn out exactly as we planned.

CHAPTER
NINE
MAL

Z eke," I shouted. "I need your help."

I stood in front of my wardrobe, having no clue what to wear. The last time I'd been out on a date, the Pet Shop Boys were topping the charts. Not that this was a date. Jason had turned me down point blank when I'd suggested picking him up. Maybe he thought it was a date too.

"What's up, bro?" Zeke sauntered in eating a bowl of noodles and lounged lazily against the door frame.

"I need your advice. I'm going out this evening with some friends, and I don't know what to wear."

"Oh, this is precious! Since when do you have friends? Is it a man or a woman? Is it a date?"

"Stop with the questions." He'd push and push until I gave him answers. Best to come clean now. "It's Jason, if you must know, and a couple of his friends. I might have intervened today when someone tried to assault him. He invited me as a thank-you."

Zeke eyed me suspiciously. "Something is definitely going on with you and Jason. First you and your demon start acting strange—don't think I didn't pick up on that—then you talk him out of the contract, and now you're going out to dinner with him."

"It's nothing. You know how hung up he is on his dead husband. Now shut up and find me something to wear." Jeez, give him an inch, and he'd take a mile. If I didn't nip this in the bud now, he'd be going on and on for days.

He put the noodles down and moved to the wardrobe, flicking through every piece of clothing I owned.

"No. No. No. No. Just how important is this date? You've nothing here post-1970!"

"Hey, it's not that bad. I bought some new suits for the job. And it's still not a date."

"Yeah, but when did you last buy anything that could pass remotely as something date-worthy?"

"It's not a date!" I exclaimed. "Just two friends having dinner."

"Except Mal the Unapproachable has none," he teased me.

He poked me with his finger, repeatedly. "Are you sure you're Mal?"

I swatted his hand away. "You're no fucking use. Go finish your noodles."

"Nah, I wanna help. This is too good an opportunity to miss. The mighty Mal fussing over clothes for a date."

I sighed. Why did he push every button I had?

"Not. A. Date. Now get out before I throw you out. Go do something useful."

He smirked, picked up his bowl and walked out, leaving me to gaze at the pile of clothes on my bed. Why was this so hard? Any other time and I'd just throw on a shirt and jeans. Why was tonight different?

Finally deciding on a dark-green shirt and charcoal-grey trousers, I left the house and drove to the restaurant, arriving at the same time as Jason and his friends.

"Mal, how lovely to see you again." Kristine leant in for a kiss. Surprised, I stepped back. What the fuck? I didn't do niceties, but seeing the look on Jason's face, I smiled and leant down, allowing the unusual show of friendship. I tried not to show my discomfort when Sam did the same.

Jason stood to the side, his gaze now on the floor.

"Jason." He looked up, and his eyes met mine. He looked great, the dark circles beneath his eyes had started to fade, and while he was still thin, he had a glow about him I'd not seen before.

"Mal." It was awkward, neither of us knowing quite what to say.

A cough startled me, and I realised I'd been staring.

"Shall we go in, gentlemen?" The amusement in Kristine's voice was unmistakable.

I'd be honest, the look on Russell's face as we walked in together was priceless. A cross between shock and annoyance. With a pinched smile, he greeted us.

"Table for four or a three and one?" Clearly he was hoping for the latter.

"Four, please, Russell. I did call and change the booking," Sam said apologetically.

"Ah, yes. I see. Come this way." He headed off at a sprint, the four of us barely keeping pace. Even with my long legs, I struggled.

I took up the rear and, on instinct, placed my hand on the small of Jason's back, guiding him. He tensed, and just when I thought he'd pull away, he relaxed into my touch.

A warmth spread through me; my demon was pleased.

Russell stopped at a small table set for four people in a small alcove. I did the gentlemanly thing and sat the ladies first. Kristine sat opposite Sam, leaving me to sit facing Jason. It was cosy, to say the least, my knees bumping his under the table.

"Well, this is…snug," Kristine said. "Are you ok, Sam? Do you have enough space?"

Sam did look uncomfortable. The alcove we were placed in didn't give much room for her protruding bump.

"I'll be fine. You worry too much." But the look on her face said otherwise.

"So Mal to the rescue today," Kristine said after we'd placed our order.

"Hardly. I was just in the right place at the right time. Brendan seemed to think it was ok to manhandle Jason. I politely told him it wasn't and suggested he leave." I shrugged. "It was no big deal."

Jason rubbed at his wrist as I spoke. I'm not sure he even knew he was doing it.

"Well, I for one am glad you were there. There was always something funny about that guy. Seems like he used his mother's death to try and get with our lovely Jason here."

She reached across the table and took his hand in hers, effectively stopping him from making it worse. I could still see a faint mark, and I seethed. Brendan was lucky he'd left when he had. There was no telling what my demon would have done.

"It was nothing, really. I'm just glad I could help him out of a tight spot."

Before we could say any more, Russell and another waitress came over with our food. Kristine and Sam had gone for a lighter option, chicken served with a mushroom sauce and salad, Jason had opted for a steak, and I had chosen the chicken but with a hot, spicy sauce.

Russell placed the plates in front of us, mine with more of a thud.

"I made yours extra spicy, sir. I hope you like it." I didn't miss the glint of malice in his eye. Little did he know, there was nothing I couldn't eat. The spicier, the better.

I bristled as his hand brushed against Jason's as he put his meal down.

"Don't hesitate to let me know if I can do anything more for you." He spoke to Jason directly, and I didn't doubt he meant more than just the food.

I had to admit it was good. Jason said his steak was cooked to perfection, and the girls seemed to enjoy the chicken. Sam, however, became quieter as the night wore on. I was no expert on pregnancy, but something didn't seem right.

It wasn't until she came back from one of her frequent trips to the ladies' room that she finally spoke.

"Mal, do you think you could drop Jason home?"

Kristine had been eyeing her with suspicion all evening, and the few times she'd asked if Sam was ok, she'd shrugged it off, saying she was fine, just a little tired was all.

"Babe, do you need the hospital or home? Just tell me." The panic in her voice was difficult to miss.

"Just take me home. I'm sure it's nothing." A sharp intake of breath said otherwise, and Kristine stood quickly and helped Sam to her feet.

"Jason, you're with Mal," she told him. He stood too, and they helped a struggling Sam out of the restaurant before he came back in, looking worried.

"Will she be ok?" I asked as he sat down.

He shrugged. "I know nothing about babies or being pregnant. I've no idea. Kristine will let me know, I'm sure."

"Should we order dessert, or do you want to go straight home?"

"Chocolate cake wouldn't go amiss. I eat when I'm stressed." He smiled tightly.

It didn't look to me as if he ate much at all, but I called over the waiter and ordered cake for him and a coffee for me. Desserts were not normally my thing.

"So, I can always get a taxi home. No need for you to go out of your way," he said while we waited.

It was no problem, and I told him so. "I really don't mind, and Sam did ask."

Conversation was stilted with just him and me, but my attention was solely on him upon the arrival of the chocolate cake. He fell on it like it was his last meal. I was captivated as he moaned around each mouthful.

Talk about food porn. My dick was hard just watching him. It was pure torture.

I gulped my coffee down, almost choking on the dregs as he forked the last piece into his mouth. The groan was sinful, and I was an expert on sin.

"Oh my God, that was so good." He wiped his mouth with a napkin, leaving a small speck of chocolate on his chin. Tempted as I was to lean in and lick it clean, I wasn't sure he'd be into that.

"It sounded like you enjoyed it." I couldn't help myself and laughed as he placed his head in his hands.

"I'm so embarrassed, but it was soooo very good. It's been a while since I've enjoyed something that much."

I was about to speak again, but the untimely appearance of Russell put paid to that. He sat in the seat next to Jason, placing his arm around the back of his chair.

"You must call me, Jason, and let me know how Sam is. Here, take my number."

Well, that was one way of doing it, I supposed.

Jason took the proffered piece of paper and placed it on the table.

"I'll be sure to let Sam and Kristine know you were asking about them. Do you think we could just have the bill now?"

"Oh, of course." Flustered, he stood and walked over to the till.

"I don't know what it is. Do I give off a 'pity me' vibe? Is this why I keep being accosted by men who think they know what I want? Be honest now."

I hoped he wasn't including me in that statement. The only vibe I'd got from him was one of grief and a deep, overwhelming sense of loss. I was attuned to it, working in the profession I did, but I certainly didn't feel pity for him.

"The only thing I got from you when I first met you was sorrow and loss. Also determination. You were determined to bring Kieran back to you."

He studied my face, looking for any insincerity, but he'd find none. I never lied. If I told you something, it was the truth. Appeasing people was not my thing, and that occasionally gave me an air of indifference. Some called it rudeness.

To be fair, I hadn't given a flying fuck what any human thought of me—until I'd met Jason.

We were interrupted again by the bill, and I fumbled for my wallet in my back pocket. Jason beat me to it.

"It's my treat. A thank-you, remember? You saved my arse today." He placed his card on the plate and smiled at the waitress as she whisked it away.

"It was nothing." If I kept saying it, he might believe me.

"It was everything. Stop saying it wasn't. I'm grateful."

With the bill paid, we stepped out into the evening. Jason shivered. Although the day had been warm, the night was much cooler.

"Aren't you cold?" he asked, his teeth chattering.

I didn't think it was quite that cold, but then again, temperature never bothered me, hot or cold.

"It's not something demons experience," I explained as we reached the car.

We got in, and I turned the heating up as far as it would go. He'd be warm enough soon, probably too much. At least we could regulate our temperature.

"Where to?" I asked him. He reeled off his address, and I put it in the satnav, realising the route would take us right past my house.

I drove in silence, just the muted sound of classical music filling the car.

"Mmm."

"What?" I asked him.

"I don't know. Kind of thought you'd listen to heavy metal or something. You know, being a demon and all."

"I listen to all kinds of music, but I prefer classical. I don't have to listen to words. I just get lost in the melody. It soothes me."

It was one of the few things from this mortal world I truly enjoyed. Not only that, but I'd befriended a few composers. They were seriously fucked-up people despite what the history books said.

We neared my house, and he spoke again.

"I wonder who lives there. I've often wondered if it's some rich bastard with more money than sense. I mean, who needs all that land?"

Amused by his comment, I turned into the driveway.

"Let's ask him, shall we?"

"God, no. Turn around. You can't go doing that to people, especially not at this time of night."

The gates swung open, and I drove straight through them, following the sweeping driveway to the front of the house.

He clutched my arm. "We cannot just knock on the door, Mal. It's not the done thing."

He looked horrified.

"I've heard he's a right bastard. Maybe he'll set the dogs on us." I laughed, imagining how Smokey would react when he saw Jason. Maybe it wasn't such a good idea, but we were here now, might as well face the music or the hellhound, as the case may be.

I got out of the car and walked up to the front door. Jason still sat in the car, open-mouthed, his eyes wide.

I raised my hand to knock when a warm hand stopped me.

"You can't, Mal," he whispered loudly. I'd not even heard him get out of the car.

"Ok, you're right. How about I do this instead?"

I got my key out of my pocket and waggled it in his direction.

"You wanker!" he said indignantly.

I laughed and unlocked the door. Yep, I was definitely that!

CHAPTER
TEN

JASON

H e'd completely played me, and I fell for it, hook, line and sinker. What I wasn't prepared for was to be knocked flat by the biggest dog I'd ever seen.

"Smokey," Mal shouted, and the dog moved off to the side and sat. Mal held out his hand and helped me up. "I'm so sorry about that."

"You," I said, barely able to finish my sentence. For one, I'd had the breath knocked out of me, and second, I was still trying to get over the fact that this was Mal's house. "Why didn't you tell me?"

"I thought it would be funny. I'm…not very good at it, sorry." The poor guy looked distraught.

"You had me going for a minute. I really thought you were going to knock!" Finally getting my breath back, I gazed around the impressive hallway. Black-and-white tiles covered the floor; there were antiques galore: tables, chairs, some beautiful rugs, and don't even get me started on the vases placed precariously within the dog's reach.

I looked towards the impressive wooden staircase, a glass chandelier hanging down, lighting up the foyer. I'd never seen a house this big. Except it wasn't a house, it was a mansion. An honest-to-God stately home.

"Do you live here alone?" Surely it was far too big for one person.

"Zeke lives here too, but it doesn't look as if he's home right now. His car isn't on the drive. I've told him how many times to put Smokey in the lobby out back." He took hold of Smokey by the collar and led him through the house into the kitchen.

That, too, was enormous with every appliance you could ever want. It put my tiny two-bedroom house to shame.

"Wow. This is some kitchen." It was all black and white, not at all like the antique-laden entrance hall. I turned in a circle, taking it all in.

"I'll just let him out. No idea how long he's been stuck inside."

Mal flicked a switch, and huge lights illuminated the rear of the house. An enormous paved area that led to acres of green.

Smokey ran outside and peed up the nearest flower pot. Poor dog must have been desperate.

"What do you do with all the land? What do you need it for?"

I was astounded that two men would need so much.

Mal shrugged. "We like privacy. We've, erm, collected a fair amount of money over the years. Made sense to us to put it to good use."

"How long have you lived here?" I couldn't remember seeing it up for sale, and I'd lived here all my life, if you didn't count the years I'd spent living away at university.

Mal waved his hands around. "A while, give or take a few years."

"Just how many years?" I was intrigued. How long did demons live? How long had Mal been alive?

"I mean, if you want specifics, probably around seventy-five."

"Seventy-five years?" I could hardly keep the disbelief out of my voice. "That's a hell of a long time."

"Tell me about it." He laughed. "Seventy-five years living with Zeke. It's been torture."

I tried doing the maths in my head but failed. There was no way he was that old. He didn't look a day over forty.

"So…" Was it rude to ask a demon's age?

"I'm old. Older than you can even imagine. Please don't ask anymore."

Shit. He looked fucking good no matter how old he was.

"You look good. I mean, for your age. Not that I'd expect you to look really old. How old are you really?"

Before he could answer, Smokey returned and started to whine, pawing at Mal's leg.

"Later, Smokey. Not now, we have guests," Mal told him, but Smokey continued, getting more agitated.

"What does he want? Don't mind me. Does he want a walk?" I couldn't imagine him strolling through Edgmund-upon-Sea on a lead. He'd scare everyone to death. The mortality rate would shoot through the roof.

"Not exactly. He wants a run, but he wants me to go with him."

"Do you want to take me home? Or I could call a taxi."

"No, I said I'd take you home." He took his keys out of his pocket, but they were knocked to the floor by Smokey. He really wanted his run.

"I can wait if he won't." I was more than happy to sit in the kitchen or maybe take another look at the many antiques the house held.

"How can I explain this?" Mal looked at me. "He wants to run with me in my demon form."

"Oh. Oh, I see." I didn't see at all. I thought… I didn't know what I thought, but it wasn't that.

I got the impression it wasn't something Mal was completely happy doing. I mean, let's face it, he didn't really know me at all. I got the impression he was uncomfortable revealing it to me, and I was fine with that.

"I can just go. Really, it's no problem." I couldn't deny I was interested to see what he looked like as a demon. Did he have a tail? Horns? Hooves? Images of Satan himself flitted through my mind. It was almost as if Mal knew.

"I don't have a tail or hooves, if that's what you're thinking."

"I… I… Ok, I was imagining hooves and a tail. Maybe fluffy legs?"

"That's a satyr you're thinking of. You've been watching too much Percy Jackson." Mal laughed, and the atmosphere lightened considerably.

"I'm not going to lie and say I'm not curious. It'd be kind of cool to see it."

I could tell he was torn between revealing his true self to me and taking me home. I had no idea which way he would go.

When he started to kick off his shoes and unbuckle his belt, I knew what he'd decided.

Smokey started running in circles, his excitement apparent.

I watched in awe as Mal revealed his toned body to me, first his shirt, then his trousers. He was all muscle with a flat stomach. Those thighs I'd admired earlier in the day were even more impressive in the flesh. And boy, what flesh it was. I swallowed, hard, as he finally stood in front of me in only his boxer briefs.

A part of me I'd thought was broken stirred. My cock twitched as it came to life. Yes, I'd wanked since Kieran had died, but it was mostly from necessity so I didn't burst. I hadn't felt sexually aroused since the moment Kieran had been diagnosed, so yeah, it'd been a while.

"Are you going to, you know." I gestured towards his boxers. Did I need to turn around?

"You're fine. I don't need to take them off." He smirked.

To be honest, he didn't need to. I could already see he was very well endowed and quite possibly half hard. He was filling his briefs nicely. Thank God for roomy trousers, he'd not be able to see the boner I was sporting.

I am a widower. I am a widower.

I repeated the sentence in my head to no avail. Nothing would deter my dick from wanting what was right in front of me. But to be honest, his demon form didn't appear to be any different. He was still the same. Was I disappointed? Maybe a little.

"Are you ready?" he asked, taking a deep breath.

So there was more. I nodded; yep, I was more than ready.

He closed his eyes, and I watched in fascination as he grew, and grew, and grew.

"Fuuuck." He was tall before, but now, he towered over me by at least a foot. Not only that, but he'd bulked out too, adding on at least another fifty pounds.

I gazed upwards. How the fuck would he get out of the door?

With no problem it seemed, as he pressed a button by a bank of full-length doors. They opened soundlessly, and he stepped out into the night.

I followed and stood watching him, gobsmacked by the transformation.

He turned to face me, a serious look on his face.

"You can't tell anyone what you see tonight. Not even Kristine."

"I won't. I promise." In all the excitement, I'd forgotten the reason why I was here in the first place and vowed to call her as soon as I got home.

Eyes closed again, Mal shimmered, blurring in and out of focus until he stood before me, resplendent with the most beautiful pair of wings I'd ever seen protruding from his back.

Almost batlike, they were iridescent in appearance, glimmering in the moonlight, the tips of them almost brushing the ground.

I reached out to touch them, eager to feel the texture. Would they be cold or warm? Soft or rough? I was fascinated by them.

It was then I noticed the black horns jutting out of his head. They were subtle, and at first glance, I'd missed them.

"You're…beautiful," I whispered, unable to find the right words to explain the vision before me. It was so much more than I'd expected.

"I've never been called that before. Terrifying was one word."

"Then they weren't looking at you closely enough." I took a step nearer to him. "Can I touch them?"

He looked startled at my request but turned his back, offering them to me.

Tentatively, I stroked the leathery wings, feeling them quiver beneath my fingertips.

A strangled moan left Mal. Had I hurt him?

"I'm sorry. I didn't mean to hurt you."

"You didn't." His voice was strained. "No one has ever touched me like that before."

"I can stop," I offered.

"I'd rather you didn't." His voice had deepened too. There was a hint of an underlying growl that shot straight to my already rock-hard cock. This was the demon I never thought I needed.

With both hands, I caressed each one in turn, not missing an inch of the surprisingly soft membrane. He stumbled, and I caught his arm before he could fall.

Shit, he was heavy, and I struggled to right him.

"Thank you." That growl again. It did things to me I'd never imagined before in my very sheltered life.

"Are they just for show, or do you fly too?" It might have sounded like a stupid question, but how was I to know they weren't just for show.

He took five strides and was airborne, gliding through the air, only flapping his wings intermittently. He was silent, not a sound coming from him. Smokey bounded about on the ground and chased after him, excited to see his master in the air. He yelped and howled. No wonder they lived so far from everyone. He was enough to wake the dead with that racket!

Completely awestruck, I tracked his path as he flew towards the tree line, disappearing from view mere seconds later. His wings gave him excellent camouflage.

I continued to scan the sky, looking for him, but all I could hear was the sound of Smokey crashing through the trees. I stepped out onto the soft grass and turned 360 degrees, my eyes skyward, gazing into the inky darkness.

Nothing. Not a sound. Unsure on how long he'd be, I walked to the comfortable chairs on the patio and sat, no longer cold. Seeing Mal transform into his demon had definitely caused all kinds of heat to course through me, and my erection still pressed against the confines of my trousers.

I had some time to reflect on how I was feeling. Never in my wildest dreams did I think I'd feel this again for any man, let alone a demon. Yet here I was, fantasising about his hard body. Now I'd seen it, there was no taking that back. His image was ingrained in my mind, probably until the end of days.

"You look deep in thought." I jumped, not having heard him approach.

"I was just thinking…" I didn't know what.

"Anything you care to tell me about?" His deep growl filled me with an overwhelming sense of lust. Was he doing that to me, or was it an unconscious reaction to something I didn't know I needed? His scent filled my nose. It was divine, a mixture of sweet and spice, and I melted.

I swivelled in my seat and looked up, straight into his eyes. Not the usual deep brown I was used to, but gold, glowing in the darkness.

I lifted my hand and touched his face, trailing my fingers down his cheek and along his jawline. A low rumble emanated from him, and he leant into my hand, feline in his mannerism, his eyes once again closed.

Temptation filled me, and I closed the distance between us, brushing my lips against his. He slid his huge hand through my hair and rested it on the back of my neck, pulling me closer. I opened my mouth on instinct, our tongues twisting and tangling, breath ragged.

I'd been starved of touch and affection for so long; I was impatient, needing more from him, wanting everything he could give me. It'd never felt like this with Kieran, this urgency to take it to the next level.

And just like that, the mere thought of his name brought me crashing down to reality, and I pushed Mal away, turning from him.

"What's wrong?"

"Can you take me home, please? I can't do this. It's too soon." I began to shiver, cold settling in.

He didn't argue, but I could tell I'd upset him by the way he stalked into the house, his demon form having disappeared.

Way to fucking go, Jason, I thought to myself. Except it wasn't right. This thing that had been building between us wasn't what I wanted. I'd wanted Kieran back and had been prepared to do anything to make that happen.

So, why did I feel so shitty?

I'd led Mal on, let him think there was something between us when there could never be. He was a demon, not my dead lover.

The problem was, I had wanted him. I'd have gladly rolled over and given everything to Mal, and that had scared me, the fact that I was willing to do that so soon after Kieran's death. Kristine would have been on the side cheering me on, but I couldn't sully the memory of my husband with a quick fuck over some garden furniture.

Realising how uncomfortable the ride home would be, I called an Uber and walked around the side of the house. I started the long walk down the driveway to the road. With a little luck, now the decision had been made to let Kieran rest, there'd be no need for me to run into Mal or his brother again. I would go on with my life, alone, as God had clearly intended me to.

CHAPTER
ELEVEN
MAL

"Jason, get in the car." I pulled up beside him as he walked down the drive. I wasn't entirely sure what had happened, but I gathered it had something to do with Kieran. Guilt at how he'd acted, what he'd been feeling. He might have thought he could hide his erection from me, but demons had a sixth sense when it came to sex. I could scent arousal a mile off, and especially that of my supposed mate.

Was I annoyed? Kind of. Did I understand his hesitancy? Also, yes, it didn't mean I liked it.

He carried on walking, not breaking his stride. "You can't walk all the way home. It'll take forever," I said, driving slowly beside him.

"I ordered an Uber. It'll meet me at the end of the drive."

"For fuck's sake, Jason. I promised Sam I'd take you home, and a demon never breaks their promise. Now stop being stubborn and get in the damn car."

He stopped and came to a decision. He opened the door and slid in beside me.

"Only because you promised Sam. No other reason."

I nodded and drove as he fiddled around with his phone, presumably cancelling his ride.

"Look, about before," he started.

"It's fine. It doesn't matter. I understand why you stopped." I did, but trying to calm my demon after being so wound up had been difficult. Since meeting Jason, my usual iron control had been slipping, the urge to shift stronger than ever.

"It does matter. I led you on, and that was unfair. I wasn't ready. May never be."

I didn't think that was true. He'd been the best I'd seen him tonight, and I truly believed he was starting to at least live a little more. I could wait, but not forever. Nobody had forever.

"Look, I get it. You don't think you'll ever get over him, but give it time." I had plenty more years in me.

He fidgeted uncomfortably in his seat, and I didn't miss when he swiped at his eye. Decisions were fucking hard, especially when they involved the heart.

"I really thought I was ready."

Taking a chance, I reached across and placed my hand on his knee. As before, he tensed, then relaxed.

"You'll get there. I promise." Not wishing to push further, I put my hand back on the steering wheel and drove the rest of the way in silence until we got to his house.

It was a tiny, detached, old house. An overgrown garden out front, illuminated by a small light next to the front door.

"Well, this is me," he said with a sigh. "Thanks for bringing me home."

"You're welcome." Should I get out too? Walk him to the door? Was that too much? I had no idea about these things, but by the time I'd made up my mind, he was already at his door. Decision made, I jumped out quickly and reached him before he had time to go inside.

"I had a great evening, and thank you for the meal." I held out my hand for him to shake. What did one do in these kinds of situations?

He chuckled as he looked down but took my hand anyway.

"It was my pleasure." He shook, then surprised the fuck out of me when he leant up and kissed my cheek. "I'll see you around some time, Mal."

Before I could even utter another word, he was inside the house. He closed the door gently, his eyes never leaving mine until finally, all I could see was his shadow through the glass as he moved away.

As unexpected as the chaste kiss had been, it gave me some hope that all was not lost. Maybe I needed to court him. Was that what people did? It had been so long; I'd lost touch, and as I drove home, I put a plan in place.

He was my mate, and my demon needed him.

THREE DAYS HAD PASSED, and the only contact I'd had with Jason was him texting me to tell me that Sam was fine, the baby was fine and all was good.

Unsure of how to respond, I'd sent him a 'thumbs-up' and the word 'Great'. My mad seduction skills needed work.

There was no point asking Zeke for help, and for as much as he teased me about dating, I didn't remember the last time he'd dated anyone, preferring to fuck 'em and leave 'em, as he so eloquently put it.

I was sitting in my office, waiting for the next client of the day, when the buzzer on the door sounded. The last time that had happened unexpectedly was the day that Jason had walked into my life and turned it on its head.

This time, however, it was Kristine.

"Hi, how's Sam?" I was getting better at this interaction business, and actually, I was feeling some kind of fondness towards this woman and her partner. Something that wouldn't have happened a few years ago.

Maybe I was getting soft in my old age.

"She's good, and thank you for taking Jason home. We were both worried sick about the baby and kind of left you to it."

I gestured to one of the chairs in my office, and she sat.

"What can I do for you today?" If all was well, why was she here?

"I wanted to ask you what happened, you know, after we left. Jason has been a little off since then, and I wondered if anything had been said, or maybe it's something else?"

"I can assure you, I would never do anything to upset him." I was slightly perturbed by her suggestion that I'd be anything other than chivalrous. Let's face it, he'd kissed me first.

"I didn't mean that. He's kind of slipped back into his morose phase. Gazing out of the window, losing track of time. I'm worried about him and wondered if you knew why."

How much should I tell her? It wasn't in my nature to kiss and tell, so I shook my head.

"Nothing out of the ordinary. We had dessert, stopped off at my house, then I took him home. That was it."

"Do you think you could reach out to him? I have my hands full with Sam at the moment. Everything is fine with her, but the doctor says she needs to rest. Her blood pressure is a little raised, and we're just erring on the side of caution right now."

"I'm not sure I can help." I was probably the last person he'd want to see, but she didn't know that.

"You see, I think you can. He's never really had any male friends, not even before Kieran and, forgive me if I'm overstepping here, but I think you could be just what he needs. I won't lose him again to his grief. I can't go there again with him, and as I said, with Sam...I have my hands full."

"I mean, I can try. Perhaps I could stop by the shop later? I have a client shortly, but could we have coffee again?"

"Yes! That would be amazing and actually takes a lot off my

mind. I'd best go. I told him I needed to grab a few things for Sam. Not exactly a lie, but I should get back."

I nodded and she stood, hesitating at the last moment. "Just be his friend. He needs that."

With that, she was gone, leaving me to my own thoughts on how I was going to do that.

The rest of the morning flew by. The clients, a man and his daughter here to bury his wife, were suitably grief-stricken. And whereas before, I'd have been all business, today I took the time to listen, and it made me realise what Jason had been going through.

I sent them off as happy as they could be, promising them to give them the best service possible, and for that, they were grateful.

It was just after lunch, and my demon was itching to get to Jason. I grabbed his favourite coffee and headed on over to the shop.

He looked up as I walked in, surprise on his face.

"I didn't expect to see you here," he said.

I handed him the coffee. "A peace offering."

"What for? You didn't do anything wrong. That was me." He took the coffee and sipped it. "How come everyone knows what I drink? I'll be having words with Harry."

Harry had indeed told me what Jason drank, and I'd stored it away for future reference.

"Can we start over? I can't help but think I scared you away with the whole demon thing."

"It really wasn't the demon thing." I scented his arousal again. The mere mention of my demon was turning him on.

"Maybe not, but I do have a proposition for you. You run an antique shop, I have lots of antiques. How about you come to the house and take a look? I'm looking to sell some of them and wondered if you'd be interested in first refusal."

"I couldn't afford to pay you for them, Mal. Some of those were priceless, I'm sure."

"I have some tucked away that might be of interest to you. Say yes, and while we're there, I can make you dinner. I don't have much in the way of friends, and I don't think you do either. We have an interest in common. Why not meet up to talk about it?"

It was the lamest excuse I could come up with, but Kristine had said to be his friend. I couldn't go barrelling in, telling him he was my intended and I was struggling to keep my demon in check.

Jason hesitated, then grabbed his keys. "It's like a grave here today. Let's go. I can follow you in my car."

"We'll drop yours along the way and take mine."

"Sounds like a plan."

TWO HOURS LATER, Jason was surrounded by the antiques I'd found for him. Some I knew would be worth a fortune. Some, not so much. He was like a kid in a toy shop, and his face lit up even more when I brought out another.

"Where did you even get this stuff?" he asked, turning over a piece of Wedgewood in his hands.

"I bought a few; others were gifts. You're welcome to any of them."

"Oh, I couldn't. I don't have the money to buy them from you." He looked thoughtful for a moment. "I could put you in touch with someone if you really wanted to sell. We have loads of contacts in the trade."

In truth, I only wanted Jason to have them, and I didn't have so much interest in selling.

"Look at the time; we should get dinner started."

I offered him my hand and helped him to stand, that all too familiar frisson of electricity passing between us.

"I don't know why that keeps happening," he said, shaking out his hand.

We made our way to the kitchen where Mrs Gold was just putting the finishing touches to an apple pie she'd made.

"Malcolm, I've put dinner in the oven. It should be ready soon. The pie here will take thirty minutes. Don't leave it to burn like your brother does."

She slipped on her coat and grabbed her bag.

"It was so nice to meet you, Jason. I'll certainly be stopping by your shop."

"I look forward to it," he said, smiling.

After she'd left, Jason turned to me accusingly. "You said we'd be starting dinner. Looks like Mrs Gold has already done it."

"I had plans, but she thwarted them at the last moment. She hates it when I mess in her kitchen." I shrugged. "The offer was there, though."

All the while I was talking, I'd poured us both a glass of ice-cold water. I'd offered something stronger, but he'd declined.

We took it outside onto the patio, the late afternoon sun settling over the trees. It'd be dark earlier than usual with summer racing towards autumn.

"It's so beautiful. I could stay here forever and look at this view."

I watched as he drank, contentment on his face. He did look happy, the stress and tension I'd seen recently had left him.

"You're welcome to visit any time."

"Oh, I couldn't just turn up uninvited. What if you were, you know, doing demon stuff?"

"I can assure you, the demon stuff is usually Zeke, and it takes place late at night."

"Really? Oh… Oh. I see what you mean."

I laughed as colour tinged his cheeks when it finally clicked what I was referring to.

"No one important in your life?" he asked after a few moments.

"Not for a very long time. I'm happy being on my own." Until two weeks ago, that would have been true, but since meeting Jason, my stance had changed. I was no longer content.

"I thought that, until I met Kieran and I was smitten from the moment I laid eyes on him. Before I knew it, he was ripped from my grasp."

"You can never predict the future, Jason. You of all people know that. Sometimes it's best to live in the moment, not in the past. No one is saying forget, but don't waste your own life grieving for a lost one."

I wasn't sure if I'd overstepped again, but the timer on the oven saved me, breaking the silence.

"That'll be dinner. Would you like to eat inside or out?"

"Oh, inside definitely. I'm like a walking snack for mosquitoes at this time of night. It's like an all-you-can-eat buffet!"

We stepped back inside, and I closed the doors, turning on the AC. He sat at the breakfast bar and watched as I served up dinner.

I put a plate of food in front of him with roasted vegetables, Mediterranean chicken and mini roasted potatoes.

"This looks good. She looks after you well."

I poured us both a glass of wine and sat next to him.

"She sure does. I don't know what we'd do without her."

"Russell told us you had wild parties here," he said with a smile. "I can't picture it for some reason."

"People will always talk about the people that live in the 'big house', but I can assure you, nothing nefarious happens here. We've learnt to keep ourselves to ourselves. I just wish Zeke would remember that sometimes."

We ate in silence for a while before he spoke again.

"Is Zeke a player?"

"Oh, the worst. He says he's a lover, not a fighter." I shook my head. He couldn't keep it in his pants if he tried.

"And what about you?" Jason's question startled me, and I wondered how to answer him.

"I guess I'm neither. We don't fight really, not anymore, and it's been a while since I was anyone's lover."

"You must be lonely." He'd finished his dinner, and I felt his eyes drilling into me.

"Sometimes." The conversation was getting tense, and I wasn't sure where he was going with it.

Easier to change the subject. I stood and collected the now empty plates.

"Dessert?"

CHAPTER
TWELVE
JASON

S pending the afternoon in Mal's company, chatting and laughing with him, I realised just how much I'd missed a man's company. I wasn't going to jump into bed with him, that's not what I meant, but he was different from anyone I'd ever met.

His knowledge of the antiques he'd shown me was far superior to mine, and I sat listening to him as he told me of their provenance, his deep voice almost lulling me to sleep at one point. Not that he was boring, but it was soothing.

We ate and had a couple of glasses of wine. I wasn't drunk, far from it, but I felt more confident than I had in a while.

He'd served the apple pie with a huge dollop of fresh cream, and I felt his eyes on me as I ate each mouthful. I was unable to keep in the moans of delight. It was divine.

I dropped the spoon in the bowl and leant back on the low-backed stool.

"Mrs Gold is pure gold. That has to be one of the best pies I've ever tasted."

I looked over at him, and the glimmer I'd seen in his eyes before was back. I stumbled over my words, taken in by their brilliance.

"You have some cream, just here." His voice was low as his thumb brushed the side of my mouth, and my tongue flicked out on instinct, catching it.

He withdrew and sucked it into his mouth, swirling his tongue around the tip.

Jesus H Christ. Such a simple act had my dick swelling.

He inhaled deeply, and his eyes glowed brighter, a low growl rumbling in his throat.

I couldn't take my eyes off him. The air crackled with electricity, an energy building, to what I didn't know.

"Breathe, Jason." I let out the breath I'd been holding and sucked in another, the scent of him filling my nose; sweet, spicy…intoxicating.

My fingers brushed the hair on his jaw, a blue spark shocking us both. I didn't withdraw, though, letting my hand stroke the softness of his beard. I moved my hand higher, running it through his hair, marvelling at the thickness, each strand feeling like silken threads.

"What are we doing?" I whispered, unable to stop the feeling of want bubbling inside.

"Don't think. Just feel, Jason."

I did just that, moving to stand between his legs, his eyes level with mine. We were so close, our lips a hair's breadth away. He was like a furnace, heat emanating from his strong body, igniting a fire inside of me.

Guilt began to infiltrate my mind, but I pushed it away. As much as I loved my husband, he was gone. I was here, and so was Mal, willing to give me what I now craved.

The touch of another man.

Today had been perfect, and I'd come to the realisation I could live again, that my life hadn't ended when Kieran's had.

He placed his hands on my waist and drew me closer. I felt his hardness against me, long and thick.

He shifted again, his lips tantalisingly close, his solid erection next to mine. I closed the distance and kissed him, placing my arms around his neck, running my hands through the hair at his nape. His tongue took control, tangling with my own as his arms surrounded me. His hands moved lower, grasping my buttocks, squeezing them, bringing me closer to his cock.

I leant back, needing to catch my breath, and his lips trailed down my neck, nipping and sucking as he went. He licked my Adam's apple, and it was my turn to growl, my body singing from his touch.

"You like that?" he murmured against my skin. I shuddered. My release was already close.

I moaned as he continued caressing my arse, and all the while my cock pulsed. I knew I'd be wet with precum, and I desperately sought friction to bring myself off. I wanted to see him though, all of him.

I pulled back, drunk from his kisses. "I need to see you."

"Open your eyes, Jason. I'm right here." He covered my mouth with his again, dominating me. I lost myself to him, forgetting everything as he kissed me, hot and heavy.

I stepped back again, overwhelmed by the sensations running through me. His eyes still glowed gold. I placed my hands on his chest, trying to catch the breath he'd stolen.

"Just...wow!" I'd never been kissed like that before, and as I squeezed my cock through my trousers, he eyed me with lust.

"Keep doing that, and I'll be ripping the clothes from you." My long-buried passion flared, and I started to undress. He didn't need to rip them off; I was more than willing. I was still conscious of my thin body, but he didn't seem to care. His nostrils flared, and slowly, he increased in stature, to the height of his demon form.

I gasped. That's what I wanted to see. He undressed too, this time removing his briefs, revealing the most perfect cock I'd ever seen. He stood tall on powerful thighs, a foot taller than my five feet ten. He was a giant, and a fucking sexy one at that.

His cock was cut, long and thick, and my arse clenched at the thought of it sliding in, stretching me wide.

It'd take some prep, but I yearned for it right now.

I stared at him, my eyes wide. I was still in my boxers, eager to take him in my hands.

He stalked towards me, and my heart picked up the pace. I was excited, nervous and full of trepidation, but my arousal overtook every thought.

I quickly stepped out of my briefs, and my cock stood proud. He stopped in his tracks, falling to his knees before me, gripping my dick in his huge hand. I almost came there and then. It'd been so long since anyone had touched me.

He looked at it as if it were a snack, and when he swallowed me down in one, I yelled.

"Fuuuuuck." He gripped my arse with his other hand, thick fingers sliding down my crack to tease my hole.

I was ready to come. He released me with a pop and stood before picking me up and throwing me over his shoulder.

"Bed, now. If I'm going to fuck you, it'll be there."

Were we fucking? I'd sworn I wasn't going to jump into bed with him.

He carried me as if I weighed nothing, loping up the stairs two at a time until we reached a door. He turned the handle and kicked it open, revealing an enormous, ornate four-poster bed that dominated the room, covered in rich gold and red covers.

He placed me gently on my back, and his eyes continued to glow brightly, hypnotising me. He lay over me, taking his weight on his elbows.

"I don't know why I feel this attraction to you, but I can't help myself when I'm around you. This urge I have to touch you, care for you, make you mine."

I had to admit I'd felt an attraction to him the first time I'd met him, and I'd wondered if he was the reason I'd decided not to go ahead with my plan to bring Kieran back. A nagging doubt at the back of my mind.

And now here we were, naked on his bed. I was ready to give myself to him and, surprisingly, had zero regrets this time.

He nuzzled into my neck before nipping it with his teeth. "I want to mark you, show everyone you belong to me."

I turned my head, baring my neck to him, giving him full access. He licked, sucked and bit, then did it all over again. He was definitely leaving his mark. Unsure what to do with my hands, I raised them above my head, stretching out beneath him.

He sat back on his heels and straddled my thighs, tenderly stroking my flesh. I'd thought a demon would be strong, possessive even, but it was almost as if he revered and worshipped me.

"Touch me," I whispered, unable to take the teasing any longer.

"Soon," he growled. He took hold of himself and stroked his cock in slow, sure movements. A steady stream of precum dripped from the end, and he gathered it before placing his fingertips on my lips, letting me taste him.

I wouldn't last much longer. The wait was excruciating.

"If you don't do something soon, I'll die."

Within seconds, I was on my front, my dick squashed between me and the bed.

Hard hands, all tenderness gone, kneaded my buttocks. He spread my cheeks wide, exposing my hole to him. Warm breath ghosted over it before he licked a stripe from my balls to the base of my spine.

"I'm not going to fuck you tonight, but I will…soon."

I wasn't ready to be fucked, but I was ready for an orgasm or two. He didn't disappoint as he continued to rim me, inserting his tongue into my wet hole. He tongue-fucked me before slipping in a finger, then two until I lost all sense of time, drowning in the sensations.

He flipped me again, and leant down to kiss me, all the time thrusting his fingers inside me. I writhed in ecstasy, loud moans and breathy gasps, desperate now to release the orgasm that had been building. My balls tightened. I was going to come. Sensing the urgency, he placed his lips over my cock, and I shot my load, spurt after spurt filling his mouth. He drank it down, swallowing around me, draining me dry. It was the best orgasm of my life.

Stars burst behind my eyelids, and when I finally opened my eyes, it was to see Mal wanking furiously. I watched in wonder at the size of him and was helpless when his orgasm hit.

He roared loud enough to rattle the windows as he shot his load, his cum landing on me. Warm, sticky liquid coated my stomach and chest, and I licked my lip as a droplet landed. Pure nectar. He scooped some off my stomach and fed it to me, his eyes almost black now, pupils blown wide.

I couldn't get enough and lapped at his fingers, licking them clean.

"That's good," he crooned. "Next time, I'll shoot down your throat. Don't want to waste it."

I nodded eagerly. I'd not even had a chance to touch him this time around. I wasn't missing out next time.

Next time. There was a thought, one I never imagined I'd have.

He flopped down next to me, staring up at the canopy. I turned to look at him, watching the sweat drip down his face, his chest heaving from the exertion.

"Tell me about your demon."

"What do you want to know?"

"All of it? What does it feel like? Is it like having a different person inside of you? Why did you strip off the other night before turning, but tonight, you didn't?" So many questions running through my head.

"It's a part of me, not so much a different person, but I can sense emotions and feelings. It doesn't speak to me, but it can make its thoughts known, and if it needs to shift, there's little I can do to stop it.

"It's like a burning or an incessant itch that won't go away until I release it. Sometimes, it's a full shift; the wings, horns, etc., other times, partial, like tonight."

"So you're not like The Hulk? Your clothes won't end up in shreds?"

He laughed and shook his head.

"No, my clothes accommodate my demon form, but sometimes I need to feel free of everything, so the clothes come off, especially if my demon wants to fly. Less wind resistance."

He turned onto his side and trailed his fingers gently down my stomach, through the pool of our cooling, mingled cum.

"I should clean you up. Most ungentlemanlike behaviour, leaving you like that."

He went to move from the bed, and I stopped him.

"I don't mind. I just want to lie here for a while longer before I have to go home."

"You don't need to. You could stay the night. I could drop you home on my way to work tomorrow."

Truth be told, I didn't want to be here when Zeke turned up, whenever that might be. I didn't think he'd judge me, but I wasn't ready to take that chance.

"If it's alright with you, I'm not ready to stay the night." Doubt was beginning to creep in, regret at what we'd done this evening.

As if sensing my feelings, he brought my fingers to his lips and kissed them tenderly.

"It's ok, you know. We didn't do anything wrong tonight. Far from it. I don't want you to go home and overthink it. Will you promise me not to do that?"

He was right of course, but I knew it'd take time for me to

come to terms with the fact I'd been with another man tonight. A demon, no less.

"Come on, I'll let you shower, then take you home."

He hopped out of bed, and once again, I couldn't take my eyes off his perfect form. His muscles rippled as he walked, and that arse? I couldn't wait to touch it. I followed him into the bathroom. He was respectful and didn't try to make another move, allowing me to shower alone. I appreciated the gesture, too full of my own thoughts. I towelled myself off, and by the time I walked into the bedroom, he was already dressed, my own clothes lying neatly folded on the bed.

I dressed quickly and checked my watch. It was a little after ten, later than I thought, but I was exhausted and ready for my bed.

We said very little on the drive home. Mal didn't push, and for that I was grateful, too much in my own head.

When he pulled up outside my house, it was all I could do not to bolt for the door, but I wasn't a child. I was a grown man and needed to act like one.

Mal must have been expecting a brush-off and seemed surprised when I took his hand in mine.

"Tonight was…unexpected, but not unwelcome. I'm probably going to need a couple of days to assimilate what happened, but I promise you, I *will* be in touch. Would that be ok?"

He could do one of two things. Tell me it was ok, or tell me to fuck off. I waited with bated breath.

"Call me when you're ready. I'll be waiting for you."

I leant across the centre console of the car and kissed him. He responded as I'd hoped he would. I pulled back, not wanting to make out in front of the neighbours, and there was every chance of that happening if I didn't get out of the car now.

"Good night, Mal, and thank you."

He stayed until I was inside my house, and I heard the throaty roar of his car as he sped away.

I lay in my bed later that evening, unable to sleep. The night's events played over and over in my mind. I realised my life didn't need to end with Kieran's passing. I had a chance at something more, and I was determined to grab hold with both hands.

CHAPTER
THIRTEEN
MAL

Zeke hadn't come home last night, but that wasn't unusual. It was also Mrs Gold's day off. I grabbed a quick breakfast and headed to work. I had another meeting with Dad to discuss numbers, but business had been incredibly slow and I considered contacting Yanni. Maybe his idea wasn't so bad after all.

I scented the air as I left the house, inhaling deeply. Something was out there. My demon could sense it. The house and grounds were protected with charms and a couple of spells at the insistence of our mother. Anything undesirable wouldn't be unable to come within ten feet of the property before getting a nasty shock.

I could still sense it on the way to work and was ready for whatever it was, on high alert as I stepped out of the car. I saw nothing untoward, but as I approached the rear door of the parlour, a demon appeared, shimmering into view. Powerful enough to take out a lesser demon, he was no match for me. What the hell did he want?

"Why are you here, and what do you want with me and my brother?"

He took a step closer, and I bristled. He wasn't exactly a friendly demon.

"I'm not here for your brother. Lord Bael demands your presence in the other realm."

What the fuck was he doing working for Bael, and when did he become a lord?

"I'm going nowhere with you, and I'd like to see you try and force me."

My demon simmered beneath the surface, ready to shift at a moment's notice.

He inhaled deeply, a look of disgust on his face.

"His scent covers you. I can smell the sex from here, although it doesn't appear you have completed the mating yet. It's faint but definitely there."

I'd showered last night after taking Jason home, but as I could sense arousal, any other demon could do the same.

"It's no business of yours. Why does Bael want to see me?" We'd parted ways aeons ago.

"He wishes to take you as his mate. That's all I've been instructed to tell you. You have seven days to present yourself to him of your own free will. If you do not yield, I will be back… with reinforcements."

Before I could say more, he disappeared.

Well, fuck. That was unexpected.

Bael was the reason I trusted no one. As a relatively young demon, just a few centuries old, he'd taken me under his wing when I'd had the inevitable falling-out with my parents as most offspring do. Death and destruction were the only things that interested me. The demon realm had been a very different place then.

He'd shown me love and that not all demons were bad, and some were very good indeed.

Soon, though, his interest had waned, and I became a pet for him to play with when no one else was around. For a while, I endured it, still eager for attention until the day I found him fucking my sister.

Red was the only colour I saw, and we fought, a fight lasting days. I'd like to say I had the upper hand, but I was no match for him. He unleashed his fury, burning me in the process.

I left, hurt both emotionally and physically, and made my home in the human realm. I roamed the world: killing, maiming, taking out my uncontrolled rage on anyone that angered me, and some that had just looked at me wrong. That was a long time ago now, and the world was no longer that way.

Why, after all these years, had Bael decided we were fated mates? If I had to guess, it was a power play. My parents were high up and had the ear of many, including 'the Boss'.

I needed to call Dad.

My agenda was clear today, and I could have gone home, but in light of this new development, I needed to see Jason too. No way was he ready after only one night together to hear the news he was my mate, but I had seven days in which to persuade him he was mine.

I could do it, I didn't doubt that, but I'd need help.

Kristine had mentioned they met in the coffee shop each morning before starting work, so that's where I needed to be.

I called Dad on the way.

"What's going on with Bael?"

"Ah, you've heard. How did you find out?"

"A visit. He sent someone to tell me I had seven days to present myself as his mate. What the fuck is going on?"

"Calm down, son. We're aware of it, and we've got it in hand. He has plans to try and overthrow the system, and he thinks by mating with you, he'll bring us in line. Never going to happen."

That was a relief at least, that others were aware of it.

"You know my situation, Dad. This is just bullshit."

"I completely agree. He's going through each of the powerful families, one by one, trying his luck. So far, he's had none, and he won't have any with us either. We've got your back, son, don't worry."

Was I disappointed I wasn't his first choice? No fucking way. I'd prefer to be way down at the bottom of his list of prospective mates.

"Keep me updated." The last thing I wanted or needed was to be yanked back to the demon realm right when I was on the cusp of consummating my own mating. My demon would not be happy.

I ended the call as I arrived at the coffee shop to see Jason and Kristine leaving, bumping shoulders as they walked, laughing and joking.

He'd come such a long way in the short time I'd known him, going from grief so deep to this. Memories of last night filled my mind, the image of him as he came, the look of complete ecstasy on his face: eyes closed, his perfect lips open, the breathy moan that left him.

My dick was painfully erect, pressing hard against the zip at the thought. Fuck, but he was perfect.

As if sensing my presence, his eyes found mine, and he changed direction, heading my way. Kristine stayed where she was. Thankfully, he looked happy to see me.

"Mal, what are you doing here? It's a little out of your way, I would have thought."

"I wanted to see you." No point in lying. I wasn't that person.

"Not that I'm unhappy about that, but I thought we'd agreed on a couple of days."

I shrugged. "Would you like to go out to lunch? I know this little place we could go to. It's quiet, and they serve excellent food."

"Is it your house, Mal? Although it's not quite so little." He laughed and then blushed. "I meant the house."

"I know what you meant, and no, it's not little at all." I

smirked at him. Yeah, my mind had gone there, and now I was harder than before if that was possible.

"Pick me up at one." He leant through the open window and kissed me briefly on the lips before sauntering towards Kristine, who had a look of shock on her face.

I licked my lips, tasting coffee and caramel and watched that perfect arse as he walked away. I was definitely having that. Maybe not today or tomorrow, but I would have it and make him mine.

TIME FLIES when you're having fun, or so the saying went. I wasn't having fun, and time was dragging. It was like wading through treacle.

To top it all, when Zeke walked in, the first words out of his mouth were, "Who did you fuck?"

"I didn't fuck anyone, and it'd be none of your business if I had," I responded. "Do I ask you who you fuck each and every night? No, I don't, so keep your nose out."

"I'm just shocked. It's been so long since you've been with anyone at all. I mean, literally decades, at least."

"Again, none of your business. Now, I spoke to Dad earlier." It was better to change the subject.

I filled Zeke in on the Bael situation, and his reaction was pretty much the same as mine, but he agreed with Dad that nothing would come of it, that I didn't need to worry. I contemplated telling him about Jason, deciding at the last moment I wouldn't be able to stop myself from throttling him with the inevitable ribbing I'd get from him.

"Numbers are down across the board again. I don't know what to suggest, and I'm tempted to call Yanni, as much as I don't like affecting the balance."

"About that."

"What do you know?" Fucking Zeke and Yanni. Always up to something.

"That Yanni's gone to ground. Seems like *he* upset the wrong people this time. No idea where he's gone or when he'll be back. You know what he's like. He'll be back around when it next suits him."

"Not much we can do then, unless you've any bright ideas?" I looked at him expectantly, and he shrugged.

"I got nothing, bro."

Why was I not surprised? I glanced at my computer, noting it was almost 12.45. If I was going to get to Jason by one, I needed to leave now.

"I'm going out for lunch, so lock up behind you. There's every chance I'll be out for the rest of the day."

I logged out and grabbed my jacket from the back of my chair.

"Whoa there, Malcolm. Sex? Lunch? Something's going on."

I said nothing and smiled to myself as I walked out of the office, leaving a confused Zeke behind. Let him keep guessing for a while. He'd find out sooner or later.

I managed to find a parking space outside All That Glitters, Jason leaving the shop before I even had a chance to get out.

"Someone's eager," I said as he shut the door.

"Unless you want the third degree from Kristine, I suggest we get going now."

I didn't need telling twice and pulled out into the traffic. He smelt so good and looked pretty fucking hot too in his jeans and polo shirt. I fidgeted around in my seat, trying to get comfortable. I don't think my hard-on had subsided all morning, and now he was sitting next to me, it throbbed.

He glanced at my lap. There was no hiding it, and I wasn't sure I wanted to. What I wanted was for him to whip it out and give it a good sucking. A demon could hope.

"I hope where we're going is remote," he said. I chanced a glance at his face. His eyes were still on my dick.

"Oh, I can find remote, if that's what you want." Talking was difficult at this point.

"Yes, please," he croaked.

The little place I'd planned to go to was set in wooded grounds about twenty minutes from Edgmund-upon-Sea. Fifteen minutes into the journey, where we'd eyed each other with hunger, I stopped the car in a secluded spot, hoping that he wanted this as much as I did.

"What was I thinking, telling you to wait a few days. I can't wait any longer, Mal."

In seconds, he was across the centre console, trying his hardest to get on my lap. I moved the seat back as far as it would go, finally seating him on my cock.

We both groaned as he rested his forehead on mine.

He circled his hips, his hands resting on my shoulders.

Fuck, I was going to come in seconds at this rate.

I grabbed his face and brought his lips to mine, devouring him. His hips stilled for a moment as he kissed me back, attacking me with the same ferocity, nipping and licking, biting and sucking. I gripped his arse and rocked him back and forth, his erection grinding against mine.

"Fuck me, Mal," he said, finally leaning back against the steering wheel, trying to catch his breath.

"With pleasure, just not here."

"I didn't mean that, it was an exclamation, but now I think of it. Oh, never mind. Kiss me again."

I did as he asked, both of us getting hot and heavy. He leant back again and fumbled with the fastening on his trousers.

We were too confined in the car. There just wasn't enough space.

"Get off and get out."

"What? What do you mean?"

"I mean, we need more room."

"Oh, right. I thought you were kicking me out."

I checked our surroundings as we stood in the wooded area. There was no one around, as I suspected there wouldn't be. We were far enough away from anyone to go undisturbed.

I toed off my shoes and undid my trousers, finally releasing my cock from the confines of my briefs with a sigh. So fucking good!

Jason did the same, and we stood there, looking at each other, cocks bouncing in front of us. He wasn't small, but then neither was I. I'd happily take him.

"What now?" he asked.

"What do you want? I'll give you anything." I was here to pleasure my mate and would go to any lengths to do that.

He dropped to his knees and beckoned me over. It was awkward, with my trousers around my ankles, and he smiled as I shuffled to him.

My demon was close to the surface, ready to unleash the moment I let go of the reins. Not yet, he needed to get used to me first.

Holding my cock in both hands, he ran them up and down the length. He took the end in his mouth and suckled on it, tonguing the slit. He had his back to the car, and I braced my hands on the roof, rocking into his mouth as much as he could take.

I didn't want to choke him.

His mouth was wide, and I was still only halfway in; one of his hands gripped the base, and the other teased my balls, rolling them in his hand. I continued to fuck his face, watching his obvious enjoyment. He looked up at me, his eyes watering, saliva dripping from his chin.

So debauched, but I sensed he was loving it.

I needed that arse, though. I'd already tasted it, already had my fingers inside. It was time for my dick.

"You want that fucking, Jason? You want my cock inside you now?"

His eyes went wide, and he released my dick, wiping his mouth with the back of his hand.

"I'm more than ready."

It wasn't the ideal place, but he walked to the front of the car and rested his hands on the bonnet, his stance wide, thrusting his arse into the air.

I stuck my finger in his mouth, encouraging him to suck on it. He swirled his tongue around it, coating it with his spit.

Letting go, he rested his chest on the car and reached behind him, opening his arse to me. It was a sight, clenching with anticipation before my eyes.

Slowly but with purpose, I inserted my finger, catching his prostate. He almost shot off the car, but I pressed my hand to the small of his back, keeping him in place.

Eventually adding another, I scissored my fingers, opening him up. I couldn't wait to be in there.

My cock was rock-hard and leaking. We wouldn't need lube or condoms. Safe sex wasn't something demons had to worry about; we couldn't pass on infection and with the amount of precum we produced, lube was unnecessary.

I lifted my shirt and bent my knees, getting to just the right height before sliding into him, inch by inch, until he'd taken it all.

He pushed backwards and squeezed, increasing the pressure on my dick as I seated myself, my balls finally resting against him.

In this form, good prep was all that was needed. I stilled for a moment, waiting for him to adjust to my girth.

"All good?" I asked, and he nodded, edging back a little more.

I withdrew slowly before pushing back in, over and over, steadily increasing the pace.

He braced his hands on the car again, pushing back and

clenching as I fucked him. I leant over his back and took his dick in my hand. He was hard and leaking.

"I'm gonna fuck the cum right out of you." Dirty talk was not normally my thing, but with Jason, I didn't want to hold back. "I want you to think of this later. My cock slipping in and out, and when I come, I'm going to feed every last bit of it to you. You want that?"

I knew I did, and I took from his moans that he wanted it too.

My demon was fighting now for release, and it was taking all of my control not to release him.

Mine, mine, mine. The word was on repeat in my head, increasing in intensity and volume as we fucked.

Jason wouldn't be ready yet, but his next words surprised me, and I shouted to the sky as the demon burst forth; wings and horns, and I watched as blue sparks danced around us both.

CHAPTER
FOURTEEN
JASON

I had no idea how I ended up here, in the middle of a wood, being fucked by the most perfect cock I'd ever experienced. One moment we were going for lunch, the next I was spread out on the bonnet of an Aston Martin with my arse bared for all to see.

The thing was, I absolutely loved it. Fuck consequences and fuck my inner self that called me a whore. One might argue that it was too soon, that I'd fallen on my knees for the first man that had shown me the first bit of attention, but that wasn't the case.

Both Brendan and Russell had flirted with me, Brendan making his intentions very clear. Mal, however, had crept up on me. I'd known him a couple of weeks now, and I'll admit, our first encounters hadn't been what you would call friendly, but I'd definitely been attracted to him at our initial meeting.

So many thoughts going through my head as he pounded into me from behind, I was surprised I remembered my own name.

All the while he fucked me, a word was on repeat. *Mine.*

I didn't understand, but the longer we continued, the louder the voice became. It wasn't one I recognised, and I had no idea where it was coming from. It definitely wasn't Mal.

My eyes rolled to the back of my head as Mal gripped my hips, and when he started his dirty talk, holding back became nigh impossible.

I knew what I wanted, though. I wanted his demon. I wanted demon sex. I wanted to be impaled on his giant cock. I needed it now.

"Let him out. I need him now."

An explosion of electricity shot through me as he released his demon.

I felt the stretch as his cock grew, and for a moment, I thought I'd made a grave mistake. I waited, breathing hard, my eyes squeezed shut.

"I'm sorry. I couldn't stop." Mal's deep growl sounded worried.

I reached behind me and managed to stroke his thigh, trying to tell him it was fine, that I was okay.

Slowly, I moved back, sliding his massive cock into my gaping hole. If I died now, it would be with the knowledge that I'd had the best sex of my life.

"Move." One word, and he carried on, albeit more gently than before.

I wouldn't break. I might be sore for a few days, but I'd survive and, if he was willing, I'd do it all again.

He was so big; I could feel the tip of his cock deep inside me. He brushed my prostate with every stroke, and with his hand still working my own dick, I was ready to come right this second.

Sensing I was close, Mal increased his speed and pressure. Fuck my life, I was going to die right here and now!

A cool breeze hit my hole as he withdrew, and I shivered from the loss.

"I want to come on you," he growled in my ear.

I turned quickly and lifted my T-shirt, baring my stomach to him.

"Do it. Cover me."

He threw his head back and howled to the sky. I'd never seen anything so breathtaking, so ethereal as Mal with his wings outstretched behind him. His dark hair rippled in the wind, and his cock pulsed, showering me with his release. I joined him, my own spunk mixing with his.

I watched him, completely enthralled. He was majestic and strong, horns glittering in the smattering of daylight filtering through the trees, iridescent wings shimmering. I was in awe of his beauty, for that's what he was, beautiful.

He looked down at me, a slow smile creeping across his face. He scooped semen from my stomach, and I opened my mouth in readiness as he held his fingers above. Drop by drop, it fell into my waiting mouth. I licked the air, wanting more.

"So greedy for it." And I nodded, I was starved.

He bent down and licked my stomach before kissing me, sharing our release. I'd never ever been this dirty, but with him, it seemed the most natural thing in the world.

Fully aware we were in the middle of a wood, both of us exposed, I struggled to get up from the car. Sex on a bonnet was probably the most uncomfortable place to do it, and my back twinged.

The next thing I knew, I was being swept into his embrace, his wings furling around my body, cocooning me. A feeling of safety and warmth spread through me. I slipped my arms around his waist, pulling him closer.

Mine. That voice again in my head, and this time, I knew its origin. Mal, or more likely, his demon.

"Am I yours?" I mumbled against his solid chest.

"You heard that?" He pulled back a little to look at me.

I nodded. "All the time we were having sex."

Mal withdrew and turned away from me, his wings disappearing.

"You weren't meant to hear that. It seems my demon had other ideas."

"What does it mean? I don't understand."

"How about we go for that lunch now, and I'll explain?"

I looked down at my stomach, still covered in cum, both of us partially dressed.

"I'm not sure they'll let us in looking like this." I tried to lighten the mood, sensing that Mal was having a crisis of some sort. I took off my shirt and wiped my stomach as best I could. I fastened my trousers and walked towards him, touching his arm.

He turned, a pained look on his face. "Let's go back to my place," I told him, "and you can explain. I'll make us something to eat."

I handed him my T-shirt with a shrug, and he cleaned himself up before handing it back to me. You'd think I'd be the one freaking out, hearing the word *mine* in my head, but it seemed to be affecting Mal more than me.

Yes, I'd probably have a panic attack at some stage, but right now, I was the calm one.

The journey home was a quiet one, and I anticipated him driving away the moment we reached my house, but he put the car in park and followed me into the house. I went into the kitchen first and turned on the oven. I had a frozen pizza I could throw in and was sure I could cobble together a quick salad from the bits in my fridge.

"I'm going to get cleaned up. There's another bathroom up there if you want to do the same."

He nodded and followed me. I was not used to this insecure person he'd become, and I didn't like it one bit.

I washed hurriedly and was downstairs putting the pizza in when he finally appeared, looking slightly better but still very unsure.

I grabbed us both a bottle of water and sat at the small kitchen table.

"You want to tell me what's going on? I'm not cross, Mal. I

just want to know how we went from the best sex of my life to hardly speaking."

He sat, filling the room with his presence. I breathed deeply, smelling the essence of him I'd grown used to, sweet and spice. It was overwhelming, but in a good way.

"I don't know how to explain this. I don't even know how in hell's name it happened." He hesitated, and I touched his arm gently, encouraging him to continue.

"My demon thinks you're my mate."

"Okaaay. I supposed I'd gathered that, but we hardly know each other. How can that be?"

"There's no rhyme or reason to these things. A demon just knows. I can't tell you how bad I feel about it. I get you've not long lost your husband. Hell, two weeks ago, you were all for resurrecting him. I didn't want you to find out like this. I hoped we'd have more time before I needed to tell you."

"What if I say no? What happens then?"

It was his turn to shrug this time. "I'm not sure. Dad says it could go one of two ways; either I'll go on a killing spree or fuck it out of my system."

The thought of Mal fucking anyone else settled like a stone in my gut. I didn't like that idea at all, even less than the killing spree, if that made any kind of sense at all.

"And now I have Bael wanting to take me as *his* mate. Although Dad says he has that covered."

What the fuck? Who was Bael?

"I think you should explain that." I was not losing my mate to someone else! Mate? Jesus, what was going on?

"Bael is an ex-lover from a very long time ago. He's trying to increase his standing in the demon realm, and the way he plans on doing that is by taking me as his mate. My family is of note there, so he thinks by assimilating into our family, he will have more power."

"Do you want that?" My heart was pounding, thinking he

was going to say yes, that this was the moment he told me that even though I was his mate, he was promised to someone else.

"Fuck, no. I want nothing to do with him."

Well, that was a relief. I couldn't believe I was so unaffected by his admission, but something did feel right about this whole thing. I remembered how he'd saved me from Brendan, how he'd acted in the shop, and things started to make sense, like jigsaw pieces falling into place.

The beeper sounded on the oven, but I ignored it. I suddenly didn't feel very hungry, the realisation hitting me that I was someone's mate.

Mal stood while I had my moment and removed the pizza from the oven, placing it on the worktop.

"I think it might be best if I go." He patted my shoulder as he left, and that same spark skittered between us. I jumped as the door closed behind him and was still there an hour later, the cold pizza still sitting uneaten.

What in God's name was I going to do now?

AN INCESSANT RINGING brought me out of the trance I'd been in. It was the front door, and I knew who'd be on the other side. The only person who would notice my absence. Kristine.

"What the actual fuck, Jason?"

She smacked me in the chest as she walked past me and into the kitchen. She threw herself into the chair recently vacated by Mal, a thunderous look on her face.

"I've been calling, left umpteen messages and finally, thinking you'd been left for dead at the side of the road, I called Mal. He told me he'd left you here hours ago."

Tears streamed down her face, and I handed her a tissue. She snatched it off me, dabbing her eyes.

"I thought you'd done something stupid, Jason."

I sat opposite her, and I felt the colour drain from my face. I was such a fucking idiot.

"Kristine, I'm so sorry. I just had a lot to take in today. I never thought."

"You know what, you never do lately, Jason. I've tried so hard to be a supportive friend. We both lost Kieran, and now I have this thing with Sam too…"

She continued to cry, and I realised just how selfish I'd been since Kieran's passing.

"I didn't think."

"No, you fucking well didn't. I'm so damned cross with you right now, Jason."

"And you have every right to be."

I let her cry for a while, handing her a glass of water when she'd finally calmed down.

"Now tell me what the fuck happened with Mal because so help me God, if he hurt you, I'll kick his arse from here to kingdom come."

I contemplated how much to tell her. Most was private between him and me. There was no way I was telling her about hot demon sex in the middle of the woods. Didn't mean I couldn't tell her the rest.

"It's an incredibly long story, one that you might have to suspend disbelief for a little when you hear it. It seems out there for me, and I've lived it. It started a little over two weeks ago, when I had that haircut. I met a man called Zeke, and he made me an offer I thought I couldn't refuse."

I told her the whole story: about meeting Mal, the resurrection, the contract, the whole nine yards. She listened open-mouthed, eating the cold pizza while I talked.

When I got to the part about being his mate, she gasped. "Well, fuck me."

"Kind of what I said." Except I meant it literally, but I didn't tell her that.

"And you've been sitting here ever since?"

I nodded. "Pretty much."

"What are you going to do? Seems like a big step if you ask me."

I agreed and told her that. "I'm going to leave it a few days, mull it over and see what happens. I already feel like I want to go to him, but I can't. Not yet, anyway."

"What about this Bael person? How do you feel about that?"

I laughed dryly. "Not happy, that's for sure, but why that is, I don't know."

"I should go. Sam will be waiting for news. Are you sure you're going to be okay?"

I told her yes, I'd be fine and waved as she drove away, relieved I'd been able to tell her about everything. She'd been unhappy about me wanting to resurrect Kieran, and rightly so, but said she understood my reasons for doing so, even if they were the wrong ones.

The problem was, what did I do with this now?

I needed time to think.

CHAPTER
FIFTEEN
MAL

It had been six days since I'd last seen Jason, and each day that passed put me in an even worse mood. I'd even snapped at Mrs Gold, and that was something I'd never done before.

The Bael deadline was looming, and I'd heard nothing more from Dad other than it was under control. Call me sceptical, but I wasn't holding out any hope of the problem going away.

"What the fuck is wrong with you?" Zeke asked that morning as we sat in my office.

"I'm fine."

"No, you're not, and you haven't been for the past three weeks. I spoke to Dad."

"And?"

"He told me about Jason. Why didn't you tell me? I'm your brother, Mal."

"So you could tease me about it? Never shut up about it?"

"I know I'm a dick most of the time, but a mate? That's some serious shit right there. Not something we joke about. I would have listened. I guess I've been waiting for you to tell me."

I'd obviously done my brother a disservice, but you couldn't blame me.

"It's been six days since we last spoke about it. I guess that's my answer. I'm not going to become Bael's mate, though. That shit's not happening."

"Do we need a plan? Maybe we should kidnap Jason, keep him in the basement until he agrees."

And this was one of the reasons why I hadn't told Zeke. I knew he'd come up with some fucking stupid plan.

"Just no, Zeke. If he wanted to be my mate, he'd be living here and sleeping in my bed. As it is, he's still living on his own, going to work every day." I might have stalked him a little since our last meeting. Sometimes it seemed he could sense me, as I'd often catch him gazing around, scanning his surroundings.

"How long until Bael's demon returns?"

"By my calculations, I have a day, if that."

"I'll stand by you when the time comes, and I'm sure Yanni would be more than happy to fight with us. Hopefully he'll get my message."

"I'm hoping it won't happen, but thank you, Zeke. Your support means a lot to me."

"We're brothers, that's what we do. I know you'd do the same for me."

AS MUCH AS I wanted the day to drag, it flew by and all too soon, it was the day of confrontation. I was on edge, wishing that nothing would happen, but knowing deep down that Bael wouldn't give up. He'd always been a stubborn bastard, his eyes always on the prize.

I was the prize.

Eager to get it over and done with, I left the house early that morning and drove to the parlour. Nothing untoward happened, and I went about my business, answering emails and talking to grieving relatives, grateful they hadn't appeared then.

Late into the afternoon, the air began to crackle. It was now or never.

I quickly called Zeke, telling him to get his arse over here, that I needed him now.

I stepped into the car park out back, not wishing to have the confrontation in the middle of the street where everyone could see.

Surprise turned to dismay as five demons appeared, led by Bael himself.

"My sweet Mal. How lovely to see you again." He looked around, disgust on his face. "How the mighty have fallen. I expected you to be some great warrior, and here you are, a lowly undertaker sending souls down to Hell. What a thoroughly boring existence."

"I'm not joining you, Bael. I will never be your mate. Leave now, and no one gets hurt." Such bravado for one standing alone, but he needed to know I wasn't going to roll over and offer myself to him on a platter. I'd kill myself first.

"Well, it looks to me as if you're on your own here. I don't see anyone here that could possibly help you," he said, gazing around.

"That's where you're wrong." Relief flooded me when Zeke stepped out of the building, closely followed by Yanni…and Jason.

What the fuck was he doing here? I glowered at Zeke, and he had the temerity to fucking smile at me.

He stepped forward, confident in his stride.

"This is Mal's mate. You have no right to take him if he's mated already. You know the rules, Bael."

"Mal? Mated? I don't believe it. He would never lower himself to mate with a human. I know my Mal. He detests them."

Jason stepped in front of Zeke and spoke to Bael. "That's where you're wrong. He is my mate. We've consummated the mating already. Several times, in fact."

"Way to go, bro." Zeke chuckled.

"You may have consummated the mating, but it's not yet complete. Is it, Mal? I can sense a complete mating, and this isn't one. Just one more step, I believe." Bael turned to face me, a wicked smile on his face.

Jason looked at me, puzzled. It had yet to be completed; Bael was right. We'd not got to that part. I thought we'd have more time. I'd not even told Jason what it involved.

"What do we need to do? I'll do it." Jason's gaze found mine and my demon growled.

"I'm sorry, Jason. He's right, and there's not enough time." It was a lost cause.

"It must be so disappointing for you, Mal, to be so close yet so far," Bael said, taking a step towards me, his hands outstretched.

Fucking Bael. I was ready to knock that condescending attitude right out of him.

"I'm not going with you," I told him again.

"Aw, see now that's a shame because now I'll have to kill your intended." He turned to face Jason.

Not on my fucking watch, and I rushed to stand in front of him as Bael rubbed his fingers together for the onslaught of fire I knew he was getting ready to send Jason's way. The exact same fire he'd unleashed on me all those years ago.

"You'll need to kill me first." I would not let Jason die.

"So bold and noble, the Mal I remember. Get out of the way."

I spied a ripple to my left, and four other demons appeared: Dad, Mum and two I didn't know. I watched as Mum muttered to herself, no doubt casting some spell or incantation.

"Bael," my father said with confidence. "You have been

found guilty of treason against the demon realm. I've been sent to take you back to face your punishment."

Bael laughed. "You don't have the power to do that, and it's *Lord Bael.*" This time he rubbed his hands, and I pushed Jason further behind me. This would not be pretty.

Bael's face fell as he thrust his hands out in front of him… and nothing happened.

"Not so brave now," Mum said. "I've cast a spell so you can neither perform your parlour tricks nor can you disappear. The same goes for the happy band you brought with you."

"Son, I told you we had this covered," Dad said. "You needed to have more faith."

"Cutting it a bit fine, though. Jason could have been killed, and I almost ended up in the other realm."

"You know I wouldn't have let that happen. We've got it from here. Go do what you need to. We'll transport this…this sorry excuse for a demon back to the realm and present him to the Boss. Let's see what *he* has to say about it."

Bael's face fell as his hands were bound in front of him. The demons he'd brought got the same treatment. There'd be no escaping the magical bonds placed on them.

"Mal, don't leave it so long next time," Mum said, smiling sweetly as she disappeared from view.

In a flash the rest were gone, leaving me, Zeke, Yanni and Jason.

I turned and took Jason into my arms, holding him close. That could have been far worse. Maybe I should have trusted Dad.

"Well, if there's nothing else," Yanni said, "I still need to make myself scarce."

"I'll come with you," Zeke said, leaving me and Jason alone in the car park.

"What the hell just happened?" Jason asked, following me back into the office.

"That was Bael, if you hadn't noticed, here to drag me back to the realm to be his mate." I sighed with relief, hoping that was the last we'd see of him.

"I gathered that, but what was that about us not being mates? I thought the, um, hot demon sex would have sealed the deal, so to speak."

"Hot demon sex is a requirement, yes, but there's also the matter of joining in blood and there might be a bit of biting involved."

I'd not got around to telling him those things before we'd parted ways. I'd already overloaded him with information the last time we spoke and worried this extra titbit would scare him away for good.

"I completely understand if you don't want to do that. I know what you said outside about being my mate."

"And I meant what I said. This past week, I've done nothing *but* think about it."

We'd made it back to my office, sitting on opposite sides of my desk. He stood and made his way around to me, turning my chair to face him.

"I choose you, Mal. Is it sudden? Yes. Does it feel right? Also, yes. Now, when do we get to the hot demon sex again?"

The mischievous look in his eyes left me in no doubt what he had in mind, and when he dropped to his knees, his hands reached for my belt.

Oh yes, I was definitely down for that.

WE DIDN'T SEAL the mating right then, that would have been weird, but the blowjob he gave me, I saw stars as I orgasmed. He drank down every drop, leaving me spent and eager for the next time.

"How did you get here?" I asked him and tucked myself away.

"Zeke picked me up."

"On his motorbike?"

"Yes, it was an experience. One I'm not wanting to repeat in a hurry."

"I'll take you home. But first, let's go for that lunch we planned on a week ago."

"Only if we can have a repeat performance of our detour."

"I can't think of anything better." My dick also thought it was a good idea and hardened again at the thought. I was a demon. I didn't need a rest between hard-ons.

Lunch was amazing, as was the company, and my demon preened. He was loving this. We didn't talk about mating at first, but Jason told me a little more about himself, pre-Kieran. I listened with interest, something I wouldn't have done a month ago.

Meeting Jason had been a revelation for me and had opened my eyes to humans and the realisation that even the most clueless demon could find a mate.

"So, this mating malarkey. What's next for us?"

"Do you want it, Jason? I'll not force you."

"I know that, and I wouldn't let you. I was shocked, of course, when you told me. I need to add I wasn't swayed one bit by the sex, although it was the best ever."

I had to agree, the sex had been amazing.

"I told Kristine, though, I'm sorry. I had to talk to someone about it, and I swore her to secrecy. I can't explain how, but it feels right. What I said earlier, whatever we need to do, I'll do it."

"There's no urgency now, so if you need more time to think…"

He reached across the table and took my hand. "As long as it takes, Mal, but I want to be your mate."

I took him home, and he took me to bed. He was open to

anything, and when I bit down on his shoulder, his orgasm ripped through him so hard he almost passed out.

"So fucking good." We lay breathless and boneless on the bed, neither of us wishing to move. I felt a shift in him, a sadness that washed over him, stealing the sexual high.

"What's wrong? Did I do something?" I still wasn't used to pleasing someone other than myself.

His hands flew to his face, and a gentle sob left him. Now I was really worried.

"We're in bed…our bed. Mine and Kieran's."

Still not seeing the problem, but then I was pretty clueless in matters of the heart.

"I haven't been in it since he died. I wasn't able to."

Ah, now I saw the problem. I gathered him to my side and let him cry it out. I had no solution for what had happened, other than he needed to rid himself of this anguish.

"He would understand, you know. From the little you've told me of him, he was a good man who would want you to move on. I think you know that too. I'm sorry we're in the bed, but I don't think either one of us was thinking with our heads earlier."

I heard him sniffle, then give a little laugh.

"Not this head anyway." He tapped his own head. "We were in the moment. It's no one's fault. Like his coffee cup breaking, like him dying, but then if he hadn't died, I wouldn't have met you."

"Fate is a funny thing. It sneaks up on us at the last moment, when we least expect it. Good or bad, it has its reasons."

Jason's phone rang, and he grabbed it from the nightstand.

"Shit, it's Kristine. I was supposed to let her know what happened, but I guess we got waylaid."

"Take the call. I'll go get us something to clean up."

I laughed as I heard him try to explain why he'd not called.

"Hi, Kristine. No, we're both fine. Yep, still both here. Uh-huh. I know I said I'd call, but a few things came up."

I laughed a little louder. Yes, a couple of things had risen their heads that we'd needed to take care of, and I'd gladly do that over and over.

"Yes, that was Mal laughing. Yes, it does mean what you think it meant."

Funny how I'd gone from thinking humans were the most tedious, odious things around to not only finding my mate but finding a couple of good friends in the process.

Maybe Dad had known all along. Some demons had a sneaky sense of the future, and I wouldn't put it past him to send me here, knowing my mate was just around the corner.

CHAPTER
SIXTEEN
JASON

S everal weeks had passed since Bael had appeared before
being unceremoniously dragged back down to the demon
realm. Mal had said no more about it, and I hadn't asked.
We'd had sex more times than I cared to count, but Mal hadn't
mentioned the mating again and I was beginning to think he
never would.

"So, you're no closer to sealing the deal than you were two
weeks ago. He's said nothing?"

Kristine and I sat in our usual seats in the coffee shop before
going to work.

"Not a dickie bird. I mean, I'm not saying we're not having
hot demon sex almost every time I see him."

"Ew, too much information." She paused for a moment.
"Actually, give me all the deets. What's it like? Is he like huuuge
when he's in demon form? How are you not walking like you've
been riding a horse non-stop for the past few weeks?"

"Okay, that really is more information than you need. What
do you care, anyway? You're a lesbian. I didn't think dick was
your style."

"Hey, do you actually know anything about lesbian sex?"

"Hmmm, I think I can guess." She whacked me on the arm and sat back in her chair.

"But seriously. Do you still want to be his mate?"

I'll admit there were times when this felt completely outlandish, that someone up there, or down there, was having a good laugh at my expense. That this was all some joke to the powers that be, if they even existed. Although the fact there was actually a hell suggested there was a heaven too.

And that's where Kieran was right now, watching over me… having hot demon sex!

OMFG!!

"What's wrong, Jason? You just went deathly pale. Do you need a doctor? Ambulance?"

I shook my head. "No, I just had this horrible thought that Kieran was watching me have sex with Mal."

Kristine burst out laughing. "Pretty sure that's not how it works, but that is funny."

She glanced at her watch and, as per usual, gulped down her coffee.

"I know, I know. Time to get moving," I said and signalled to Harry for my to-go cup.

"Yes, the sign man is coming today, and we've still got a load of stuff to box up."

When I'd mentioned changing the shop, what we sold and what we were called, Kristine had been reluctant. I'd left her to mull over it for a while until she finally told me she thought it was a good idea and we should do it.

Since then, it had been all systems go. We'd already sold a lot of the stock, some of it making a handsome sum, some of it barely making any at all, but it was a start.

She'd enrolled in a couple of courses, and we'd agreed to become partners…of a business nature of course.

When we reached the shop, Mal was parked outside, lounging against his Aston looking like a big ole snack.

"You know, if I wasn't a lesbian, I'd be fighting you for that," Kristine whispered as we neared him. "He's fucking hot, and he knows it."

He did look particularly good today, wearing the tight trousers that showcased his amazing thighs. His black shirt was open a little at the neck, and his hair and scruff were perfectly groomed. How had I got so lucky?

As he watched us approach, he removed his sunglasses and placed them on the top of his head. His eyes glowed gold.

Kristine fumbled with the lock before finally opening the door, leaving me outside with Mal.

I walked over and stood before him.

"You're looking particularly hot today," I said, trailing my hand down his face.

"As are you. I came by to see if you wanted to go out this evening." He bent to whisper in my ear. "There's a particularly small place I know where they serve the most wonderful food and the dessert there is to die for."

"Mmm, sounds interesting. You know how I love a good dessert." I'd discovered this fascination for eating spunk, Mal's in particular. I loved it when he fed it to me with his fingers or, better still, kissed me, filling my mouth with his release and his tongue.

I couldn't get enough, and just the thought of it now, had my dick straining for release.

"You want it bad. I can smell it on you." He looked around, seeing no one was near and took my hand, placing it on his hard cock. I felt it pulse beneath my touch. What I wouldn't give to have him fuck me right now.

I dropped my head to my chest and squeezed my eyes shut, trying to gather my thoughts. I had a whole day to get through with images of him running through my mind, always naked.

"How soon can you get off?" I asked, hoping he didn't have

many appointments today. As much as I didn't want to, I could duck out early. I was impatient for him today.

"I could get off right here and now, if you wanted me to. It really wouldn't take much. I've not had my dick up your arse for at least a day, and my demon has missed it. I've missed it."

"Fucking work, always getting in the way of things."

"Just remember how good it'll feel when I finally slide right in, my name on your lips as I fuck the cum out of you."

I was an absolute sucker for his dirty talk, another kink I'd discovered since meeting him.

I groaned, wishing it was afternoon already. "Go before I whip your dick out and drop to my knees in the middle of the street. Not sure some of the oldies would like it. You might have a few more customers if I did that; they'd die of shock."

"You know, I hadn't thought of that."

I stepped away before I followed through on the ridiculous notion and turned to go into the shop.

An arm wrapped around my waist from behind, and a voice growled in my ear. "I'll pick you up at six, and my dick will be inside you by six thirty, maybe even sooner."

The arm disappeared, and I stood on the pavement, eyes closed, and listened to the roar of his car as he drove away. That demon would be the death of me.

AFTER WHAT SEEMED like an eternity and a day where every thought was filled with Mal, six o'clock finally arrived.

We'd closed the shop around five. I drove home and jumped in the shower, prepping myself for the night ahead. I packed an overnight bag, just in case. It definitely paid to be prepared.

Mal was right on time, and I flew out of the house, almost forgetting my keys in the process.

I grabbed his face and kissed him, sliding my tongue inside his mouth, letting him know how much I wanted what came next.

Something felt different. There was a desperation in his kiss too.

"Forget the food." I reached across and stroked his length, trailing my fingers on either side of his cock, feeling it swell beneath them.

"Agreed. We'll go to mine. Zeke's out, and Mrs Gold has already left for the day. We'll have the house to ourselves."

How Mal didn't get a speeding ticket was beyond me, but I didn't take my eyes off him for a minute as he made the fifteen-minute journey to his place in just ten.

We barely made it out of the car, stripping out of our clothes as we went until we reached the staircase.

"Ever had sex on the stairs?" he said in my ear, holding me close, my back to his front. I could feel the press of his erection, and I turned to face him.

"Nope, but I think I'm about to," I said and ripped at his boxers, the need to see him naked ruling my every thought.

He grunted and spun me around. "Place your hands on the stairs."

I did as he asked. It took a little manoeuvring to get us on the right levels, but we managed it.

It had been difficult to take him at first. I'd needed a fair bit of stretching to accommodate him, but now, I hardly needed any and I moaned with pleasure as he slid his thick cock into me.

"Oh, yeah. So fucking good." He started slowly before finally picking up the pace. My hips rocked with him, driving him deeper.

The tip of my sensitive cock brushed against one of the steps in front of me, increasing the sensation.

"Do you want him?" Mal's voice was strained, and I almost didn't hear him, but I knew what he was offering me.

"I need him," I said, waiting for the shock of electricity that passed through us every time.

Mal stopped thrusting as his demon burst forth, filling me completely. My heart felt full of love and want and need, but it wasn't only mine I could feel.

He started again, and I threw my head back and howled. "Fuck, yes."

Mal's demon form surrounded me, taking over, and I embraced it, letting him in, giving in to him.

I was ready to come there and then. He was right when he said he could fuck the cum right out of me, especially in his demon form. I had no control, all of it down to him. The pressure built, his huge cock pistoning back and forth. I could hear his laboured breaths behind me getting quicker and quicker.

He was close too.

"Make me yours, Mal. Do it now." I knew what I was asking. I just hope he did too.

I felt the graze of his teeth at my neck and bared it to him, offering him all that I had.

He bit down hard, and I knew this time, he would have drawn blood.

A burst of light and brilliant blue sparks of electricity flitted around us. My body was on fire, white flames licking at my skin, yet there was no pain, only euphoria.

Was I floating? I felt weightless as Mal's arms surrounded me, the flames dancing along his skin.

"You need to bite me, Jason. Anywhere will do, but hard. The mating process needs blood from us both."

He forced his arm into my mouth. Could I do this? Damn right I could, and I bit down, a metallic tang on my tongue.

I must have blacked out, as I remembered nothing more but found myself lying in his bed feeling elated. Mal watched over me, a smile on his face.

How do you feel? he asked, but I was confused. I could hear his voice, but his lips hadn't moved.

"What the hell is going on?"

We are mated, and as such, you can hear me and I can hear you. Try it.

What should I say?

You don't need to now, I heard that.

This was freaky weird. He hadn't told me about that.

I'm sorry, mate. In the heat of the moment, there were a few things I should have mentioned.

Like you being in my fucking head!

You'll get used to it, and once you learn more, you can turn it off. You'll not want to know what I'm thinking at all times of the day and when you're discussing antiques with Kristine. You get the picture.

"So we're mates now." I spoke out loud this time. The whole mind-talking thing would take some getting used to.

"Yes, we are. There are infinitely more benefits to being mated, but we can talk about them at a later date. Can you feel this?"

His lust washed over me. I could definitely feel that. An overwhelming sensation. I wasn't averse to that happening.

"Now, I think we should do it again, but this time, let's be awake for the actual orgasm part. I think we both missed it last time."

The rest of the evening flew by in a haze of love, contentment and lots and lots of hot demon sex. It had increased in intensity since the mating, and each time, I came harder and harder. I was surprised at my stamina and recovery rate, and when I mentioned it to Mal, he said it was part of the mating, that I needed to be able to do that to keep up with his insatiable appetite for me.

I was more than happy, as I had my fourth orgasm of the night.

Three a.m. came around, and my stomach growled. In the excitement of it all, we'd forgotten to eat.

He threw on a pair of shorts and handed me a pair. I tied them as tight as I could. Although I'd put on weight these past few weeks, I was still thin.

Zeke was sitting in the kitchen when we finally made it downstairs.

"I picked up your clothes from the driveway," he said, laughing. "I guess tonight was the night, eh?"

Embarrassment filled me, but Mal cuffed him around the ear. "None of your business."

"Oh, I think it was. You lit up the house like it was the fifth of November. I wondered what was happening."

"I thought you were out?" Mal asked.

"I was going to be, but then I heard all the noise. Do you think you could make it to the bedroom next time? Spunk is a nightmare to get out of the carpet."

Oh, sweet Jesus. Take me now. I begged for the ground to open and swallow me up. I was mortified.

You'll get used to him. I heard in my head. *And if you don't, let me know, and I'll deal with him.*

Zeke nodded as I smiled. "Ah, I see you have the whole head thing going on." He swirled his finger beside his temple as he spoke.

"Yeah, it's a little bit freaky right now, but I'll get used to it."

"There's a lot you'll need to get used to." He ticked them off on his fingers. "Lots of sex, more sex, longer life."

"Longer life?" That was a new one again.

Mal shot daggers at Zeke.

"Oops, sorry. I guess you hadn't got around to telling him that yet. I'll just leave you two to it."

He left the room, and I stood with my hands on my hips, trying to look as intimidating as possible.

"About that. I might have forgotten to mention that too," Mal said sheepishly.

"I think you and I need to have a sit-down and go through all of this, Malcolm."

"I think you're probably right."

EPILOGUE

TWO YEARS LATER

MAL

Being mated to Jason had turned out to be the best thing to ever happen to me. I'd gained a mate, but I had also gained new family and friends.

Kristine and Sam were sitting in the garden of our house, laughing and chatting with Jason. Their newest arrival, Betty, lay on a rug, laughing and gurgling, and Keira was being chased by Smokey. She completely owned him, and he adored her.

Jason had moved in not long after the mating, and I'd often find him in another room, gazing at the antiques I owned. Sorry, we owned. What's mine was his and vice versa, although I'd refused to become a partner in his business. He had Kristine, and I would never have taken that away from her.

Zeke was around somewhere. He'd been acting kind of strange lately, all moody and shit. I'd not had a chance to talk to him, but if my experience was anything to go by, I wouldn't be surprised if he hadn't also found his mate.

Jason had been reluctant to sell his home at first, worried that he'd lose the memory of Kieran if he did so. I knew he'd always be a part of Jason, and if it hadn't been for him, we'd have never met.

He'd ploughed the money back into the business, buying more high-end pieces and doing exactly as he'd said he would, building it into a successful antique store, Barr and Butler.

Their client list had grown, and many now flocked to them, knowing if they hadn't got it in stock, they could source it for them, no problems.

Didn't hurt that I had an attic full of antiques I no longer wanted or needed. At first, Jason had refused to take them, but when he found out I was the anonymous seller he was buying his stock from, he gave in.

It caused an argument or two, but the make-up sex afterwards had been out of this world. The spark of electricity we'd first encountered would light up the room and definitely increased the intensity of our orgasms.

At some point, we'd realised we'd need to move away from Edgmund-upon-Sea. It wouldn't go unnoticed when he failed to grow older with everyone else. The people that mattered knew. Kristine had been upset at first, but realising Jason had found happiness and would be happy long after she was gone had appeased her.

I allowed my thoughts to filter into his mind, and he turned to face me, a puzzled look on his face.

What's going on? he asked.

I shrugged. *Just thinking about you and how you'd look good spread on the table with my head between your legs.*

You were not! He looked astounded and stalked towards me, excusing himself from his conversation with Sam.

I definitely was. I winked at him and dragged a finger up his bare arm, along his jawline and into his mouth. *I can't get you out of my head, it seems. How long until they go?*

Mal, they only just arrived. Give it a couple of hours at least.

I rolled my eyes. *If you insist, just remember what I said.*

How could I forget?

He turned to leave, and I slapped his arse, feeling his firm buttocks. Having me some of that later.

Fuck, Mal. Make sure you do that later. I might have found another 'thing' I like, Jason thought flirtatiously.

He was getting better at conveying thoughts and feelings through our link, and I was shocked at the image of his hard dick appearing in my head. Yep, definitely doing that later.

JASON

As much as I missed Kieran, I loved Mal with a ferocity I'd never thought I could feel. Maybe it was because he was a demon, but everything I felt for him was amplified: love, lust and life in general.

We had our moments. Mal still wasn't completely used to humans, despite having lived with them for centuries, and yes, that was another thing that completely confounded me. The fact he'd been around for so long. He'd still not mentioned quite how long, and as much as it used to bother me, I was okay with the fact now.

How long would I live for? That was another question we didn't have the answer to, but it was likely that it'd certainly be as long as Mal lived. Once mated, it was for life, and when one died, it usually wouldn't be long before the other did.

I occasionally wished that had happened when Kieran had passed so I didn't have to live the life I did for eighteen months. There'd been very little in the way of glimmers then, nothing but darkness, grief and loss.

For the most part, I was glad I'd survived. Mal was the light in my life, as much as he'd disagree with that. He liked being the badass in our relationship, but he forgot I'd seen him cry when Kiera was born, the same with Betty.

He put out this hard man persona, but he was a pussy cat at

heart, and I absolutely loved him until I thought my heart would burst.

I loved the house too, loved Smokey, and Mrs Gold was an absolute gem.

My life was complete. I couldn't wish for anything more to make me happy.

I looked over at Mal, fussing over Betty lying on the floor. Maybe a baby? Perhaps that would make us feel more complete. A family.

No fucking way. I laughed at the words in my head. I must have let that one slip through.

His look was one of horror, and I sauntered over to him, running my hands along his shoulders.

"I agree," I told him. "No children."

I loved Keira and Betty with a passion but was always happy to give them back. We'd babysat a couple of times to let Kristine and Sam have some much-needed time to themselves. It had only proved that neither of us was cut out to be parents.

How long until they go? he projected to me.

Soon. Just think of the anticipation as I slowly undress. I was less conscious of my body now. The weight I'd lost had come back, and I was fitter than ever. "I'll lead you with a trail of clothes, first my shirt, then my trousers before removing my boxers, letting you see me."

Mal growled, and Betty stopped moving, bursting into tears.

"Now look at what you made me do," he said, trying his best to mollify her.

Probably not the best time to tell you I'm not wearing any underwear then.

His face was a picture, and I stored it away for another day, along with the memory of today, the anniversary of Kieran's death.

I don't think he would have minded how we celebrated each

and every year. A barbeque at the house with Kristine and Sam and mind-blowing sex afterwards.

I actually thought he might be smiling down on me, finally at rest and happy.

I knew I was.

Happy to have friends who had stood by me.

Happy to have a mate who loved me unconditionally, as I did him.

Life was perfect.

Life was Mal.

THE END

ACKNOWLEDGMENTS

Once again, thanks to Ashlynn for inviting me to take part in this collaboration. I have to admit to being stuck for what to write for this one, but a thought came out of nowhere, as it usually does and The Undertaker was born!

I knew it was going to be tough to write. Loss and grief is never easy to cope with, but I wanted to show it's possible to move on. As always, I have a sassy friend to give advice. I'm fortunate to have a few of those myself.

As always, thanks go to my personal assistant, Tom. He's my rock, my emotional support person and just all-round good guy to have around. He makes me laugh when I'm feeling down and gives me a proper good talking to when I need the proverbial kick up the ass!

Thanks to my reader group for supporting me, and especially my admin/mod team; Tom, Kelly and Colleen. I couldn't run it without you!

My beta team and ARC team. I love each and every one of you, and love the chats too. You ladies rock!

Final thanks to the family, as usual. They put up with the late nights, the grumbling when it doesn't go right and the conversations that start 'so, do you think this will work?'

And to the puppies that keep me company in my new office.

Thank you to you, the readers for continuing to read my work and keep me going with your kind words. I couldn't do any of this without you.

Lots of love, Alex x

ABOUT THE AUTHOR

Alex is a disaster movie loving, tea drinking Brit that loves to travel, read, pet all the dogs, oh, and she writes some angsty MM romance to boot!

It's often dark, always gritty and definitely realistic. She covers difficult topics with sensitivity, but there will always be a HEA.

She's married and lives in the NW of England with her three grown boys and two fluffy dogs.

Dark With Heart – MM Romance Author

ALSO BY ALEX J. ADAMS

NAVA DANCE STUDIOS SERIES - COMPLETE SERIES

Dance With Me

Poles Apart

Indian Lace

LIVERPOOL BOYS SERIES - MORE COMING 2024

Saving Ziggy

Finding Beau

STANDALONES

Dancing With a Ghost – Haunted Love Series

His Dirty Obsession

One Last Wish – Home for the Holidays Series

The Lies We Tell

The Demon Undertaker – Possessive Love Series

Look out for more exciting stories and projects coming soon in 2024!

Printed in Great Britain
by Amazon

45479285R00098